A way out for all

# A Way Out For All

Three Lives

George Ashford

A way out for all

Copyright © 2020 George Ashford

All rights reserved.

ISBN:9798551539049

A way out for all

## CONTENTS

| | | |
|---|---|---|
| 1 | A Summons | Page 5 |
| 2 | Like Any Pit Village | Page 15 |
| 3 | Thérèse | Page 28 |
| 4 | Unwelcome News | Page 40 |
| 5 | The War and Coal | Page 45 |
| 6 | Poor Relations | Page 54 |
| 7 | Fresh start | Page 61 |
| 8 | New World | Page 72 |
| 9 | Sarah | Page 77 |
| 10 | The Best Chance | Page 89 |
| 11 | Flapper Election | Page 99 |
| 12 | A Poor Story | Page 102 |

# CHAPTER 1

## A SUMMONS

Shirby Colliery, Pump Level  March 1914

Paul walked across the pump room to where his jacket was hanging and took out a brass watchcase. Inside, the cheap pocket watch, protected by a piece of wadding confirmed what he already suspected; it was still two hours before he could get out of the pit. Putting the watch back he resolved not to look again for a while, it was only making the day longer. He really didn't like shifts like this, although very easy, it was also very boring and the hardest part was staying awake.

As a mechanic he had better things to do, but when the pump man failed to arrive and the foreman was looking for a replacement, he had been unfortunate to be at hand. It was rare for one of the regular operators to stay at home, but how they tolerated the job was a mystery to him. Spending their days alone in damp semi-darkness, the only compensation for a lost life was guaranteed work and the pay that accompanied the long hours.

Just as he was thinking of looking at the watch again the light of someone's lamp appeared coming towards him. This was strange because the Deputy had already been and there were never any other visitors but as it came closer he saw that it was him again. "What's up Charlie?" he asked. Charlie, never the happiest of men but looking even more miserable than usual said "I don't know what the fucking hell you have been up to, I've had a message from the boss to send you out to see him right away and I've got to fucking cover for you!" His heart sank, this could only mean trouble. The Manager had never spoken to him before, so why now?

On the fifteen-minute walk from the pump room to the shaft bottom he tried to think what he could have done wrong. Men were regularly sacked by the manager's underlings without him becoming involved, and he knew from experience that even the death of a relative would not have merited such a summons.

The manager's office was at the top of a steep flight of stairs, in the outer office the manager's clerk, Cecil Roberts sat at a desk with his back to a smoking fire, shuffling a pile of grubby reports. He was a mean looking little man with one arm, the other lost in an accident at some time; Paul distrusted the man, as did everyone else. Cecil was well aware of it and even enjoyed the fear that some of the workers had of him. "What's this about Cecil?" he asked, Cecil didn't know, but had no intention of admitting it. He prided himself on knowing most of what went on behind the scenes but this was a new situation even to him and he wasn't going to lose face with a workman. "You will find out soon enough, wipe your boots and wait over there until Mr. Maynard is ready for you" Cecil snapped and returned to sorting the papers into neat piles.

After an uncomfortable five minutes of silence the inner door opened and the Manager came out. Paul was almost certain from the look on his face that he didn't know him. "Come in here will you" he growled. Cecil started to follow them in but Maynard closed the door almost in his face. Whatever the trouble he was in, he thought it might be worth it for the privilege of seeing the hurt look on Cecil's face.

Maynard sat down at the desk and left him standing. He didn't speak immediately, and feeling more uncomfortable than ever Paul glanced around. The office was a larger, more comfortable version of the outer office with a bigger fire, bookcases along one wall and a map table that almost filled one end of the room, on it a large plan was held down with leather bound weights. He studied Maynard while he waited; he had seen him around the colliery but never at close quarters before. He was tall and slim, in his mid fifties and everything about him looked grey, his hair moustache, and even his eyes. He also noticed he had lost the tip of his left index finger indicating he had probably worked for a living at some time.

Suddenly looking up he said, "You have had plenty to do with HydraVane pumps!" Unsure if that was a statement or a question, he decided that it was a statement and said, "Yes." "Ever heard of Colonel Harrington?" this was definitely a question, he answered "No." "He is the Chairman of Shirby Coal Company, you understand, he pays our wages!" Maynard barked. Suddenly he realised that this man, who wielded power over normal mortals also had a boss that he was afraid of. Maynard continued, "He has got a job he wants doing, something to do with a HydraVane pump, I have been told to send him someone who can do it. Joe Adams says you'll do." Joe Adams was the Chief Engineer at the pit; Joe was only slightly more approachable than Maynard and had never given Paul any reason to think he held him in special regard.

Maynard stood up and said "He wants to see you tonight; he's in Nottingham for a Mining Engineers conference at the Trent Hotel. Go home get your best suit on and get there by seven thirty. Don't be late and don't let me down, not if you want to carry on working here, do you understand?" He had been about to try to find out more, but suspecting Maynard had already told him as much as he knew, thought better of putting him in the position of admitting it. "Go and see Cecil, tell him to give you ten shillings for your fare and bring back anything you don't spend. See me tomorrow afternoon and we will take it from there." He agreed and started to leave, he was part way through the door when Maynard said as if an afterthought "I think its something to do with France."

When he arrived home his small terraced house was empty; he wondered where his wife was but didn't have time to worry about it if he was to get the 6:30 train to Nottingham. There wasn't much hot water and it took ages to get cleaned up and changed into the only suit he owned and still Sarah had not returned. He scribbled a note explaining he had to go to Nottingham and had to run to catch the train.

It was 7:15 when he approached the reception desk at the Trent Hotel; the clerk gave him a disparaging look and asked what his business was. Not liking the clerk's tone, he decided to answer in a similar way, he said, "Mr. Blackburn Belcher and I've come to see Colonel Harrington, he is expecting me." He didn't often use his full surname, he had many times cursed some ancestor for inflicting it on him , but at moments like this, he minded less. The clerk didn't answer but looked down on a shelf behind the desk and after a few moments looking through a message pad said, "Yes the colliery person, wait over there and you will be sent for."

He sat down feeling shabby and uncomfortable, the rushed wash with lukewarm water had not been the best preparation for this and his white cuffs were already becoming dirty as he sweated coal dust from his pores. In spite of his foreboding about the meeting, he was relieved when after about a quarter of an hour a porter came to collect him. Shown into a small room off a corridor he found two men seated in leather chairs by a fire, drinking what he assumed was wine. Neither of them got up so he stood and waited for them to speak.

The older man said, "I am Harrington and this is Monsieur Henri Masson." Without waiting for Paul to reply, he continued. "Monsieur Masson needs someone to install a HydraVane pump at one of his mines in Carvin France. Maynard says you can do it, that right?" Paul spoke for the first time "Yes sir but I don't understand, why you need me to do it" Harrington interrupted "That's not your concern, just get yourself out there and do it, Maynard will sort out the arrangements." Before he could speak again, he passed him a large envelope and said "Give him this, its got all the details." The younger man now interjected, in a French accent he said, "Colonel do let the man speak" and turning to him said, "Have you any questions Monsieur?" He had so many he didn't know where to start but stumbling over his words he said the first thing that came to him, "But I don't speak the language Sir." "That will be taken care of" he said smiling and then forestalling his other questions he said "And you will have all the assistance you need from my manager." Harrington interrupted again "I have told Monsieur Masson that we can look after this for him and you won't fail us will you?" This was the second threat of the day and he understood exactly what his future would be like if he did. "No Sir." and as Harrington turned his back on him he regarded himself dismissed.

On the last train back to Mansfield he tried to make sense of the episode. He was feeling humiliated by his treatment at the hotel and still couldn't understand why he was involved or what exactly he had become committed to. A couple of drinks in the station buffet had done nothing to overcome the uncomfortable feeling that he was being loaned out by Harrington, in the same manner he would have lent an acquaintance a horse.

It was nearly eleven when he got home but Sarah was waiting up, unable to sleep until she knew why he had been on the unusual errand. He told her as much as he could but she was only part listening, the job details she didn't understand, and she dismissed his worries as 'lack of ambition'. She couldn't or wouldn't accept that this job was not the start of a rapid advancement in his career and that there was a real risk of trouble if he failed. That night so sure was she that he had done something right at last, she felt she should reward him, for one of the few times in their marriage, they made love at her instigation.

In Maynard's office the following afternoon the atmosphere had completely changed, invited to sit down he was handed the papers from Harrington and while he read them Cecil was instructed to bring in tea. He read quickly, not knowing how long this changed relationship with Maynard would last. There was nothing unusual about the job described, installing, and commissioning a centrifugal pump, but there was nothing to indicate why the French wanted a foreigner to do it.

Maynard broke the silence "And you still haven't any idea why they want us." When Maynard used the word 'us' he knew that both their livelihoods depended on this job and neither of them knew why. "No" he replied. "How long do you think it's going to take?" He had been waiting for this question and thinking that it looked like two weeks work he said "If that plan is to be believed and I get the help the Frenchman promised, about three weeks." "OK" said

Maynard "I'll tell them a month, to make sure we can finish in time. They want to start next week; I will try to find out more before you go. See Cecil, he will sort out transport and money for you and I'll see you don't lose anything by it." He thought privately, this actually meant he wouldn't make anything but kept the thought to himself.

In spite of the pressure from Harrington to get the project going straight away, it was the following Thursday before all the travel arrangements had been made and he caught the early train to Nottingham on route to France. Sarah had washed and pressed most of the clothes he owned, packed his small case, got up early, prepared food for the journey, and had seemed genuinely emotional when they parted.

Cecil had had to use a travel agent to arrange train and ferry tickets but only after a furious Maynard overcame his resistance to doing anything quickly for a workman. He had four weeks pay in advance and if as promised, the French paid him as well, he thought he might just make enough to clear their debt to the clubman. He had the name of a clerk in Lens who was to be his interpreter and a booking at Carvin's only hotel. In spite of this, never having been further than Skegness, he was still apprehensive.

As the train made its way to Folkestone, he again went over the information Maynard had managed to get. The Frenchman had been trying unsuccessfully to get this job done for some time and he was not the first outsider to be called in. Harrington's only response had been that 'they wanted someone to do the job not write reports about it'. He and Maynard had both smelt a rat and it was questionable who was worried most, probably Maynard, since he had to depend on somebody else to save his career.

He tried not to think about what the repercussions that embarrassing Colonel Harrington would be, instead he found himself thinking about Sarah and their marriage. A pregnancy scare had hurried them into it when she had been only just 20 and he a year older. Sarah was slim and pretty with fair wavy hair. She could be amusing and charming and made friends easily although she didn't always keep them and he had been the envy of his friends when they married.

That had been five years ago and he had known for over four it had been a mistake. They had not married for the same reasons; he wanted a friend, lover and eventually a mother for children and if he was honest, a quiet life. Sarah more than anything else wanted to avoid the kind of life her friends and neighbours had, worn out at a young age by large families and constant struggles to make ends meet. Bright and intelligent, she knew a woman couldn't do it alone. It needed the support of a husband who succeeded in his work and wanted to 'get on' just as much as she did.

Her mother had done it by pushing her father until he had become a stationmaster. He had a decent salary an imposing office at Mansfield station and people working under him. He had achieved this by cultivating useful friends, adjusting his interests to coincide with theirs and working unpaid hours when it would be noticed. This and campaigns of 'back stabbing' his colleagues had taken him from a station porter to his current position. There were plenty like him at the pit; to Paul he was an 'arseholer' that he had no intention of emulating.

Sarah had mistaken his easygoing nature for weakness and the more she pushed the more stubborn he became. Following the example of her sister and he suspected of her mother, she regarded sex as a commodity to be traded in battles of will and best kept in short supply. When after just a few months marriage he refused to begin attending the same chapel as his foreman, she withdrew it in retaliation. The reasons given for her unwillingness were many and varied and though never openly admitted, he knew exactly what was required of him. When she realised that she had gone too far, it was too late. The campaigns continued but for lower stakes, such as things for the house that they couldn't afford and he didn't think they needed. Some she won, others she lost, but the biggest loser was their marriage. Before they had been married a year, it was soured almost beyond repair.

He knew he wasn't the man who was ever going to make Sarah happy and if the bad feeling he had about this task proved correct, things could only get worse. In spite of the display of affection on his departure it was not a new start, nothing had changed and he felt sad for Sarah as well as himself.

# CHAPTER 2

## LIKE ANY PIT VILLAGE

### Carvin, Northern France

The journey to Carvin was long and uncomfortable, Cecil had made sure of that; it could have taken eighteen hours with good connections but took nearly thirty six. The route had sent him out of his way and used the slowest, most uncomfortable trains, possibly to save money or more likely to satisfy Cecil's pride.

It was early Saturday afternoon when he walked down the main street of Carvin, he was cold, hungry, and any remaining ideas of glamour attached to foreign parts had evaporated. Apart from hoardings in French it was like any pit village in Nottinghamshire; mostly single story houses and buildings with the colliery and its spoil heap at the end of the road towering over it.

The hotel did little to lift his spirits either. The reception was less than friendly and he had to wait in his cold room until seven before any food was available. When food was eventually served in the bar, he managed to order the 'plat de jour' and a beer. He had no idea what it was either before or after eating it, but was so hungry by then that he was past caring. After another beer and unsuccessful friendly approaches to a small group of men drinking at the bar, he gave up and went to bed.

The cold, slightly damp bed had not been very inviting but lack of sleep in the previous twenty-four hours caught up and he didn't wake until late morning. It was Sunday and he had all day to kill, the interpreter was to meet him the following day and take him to the mine. Finding it was too late for breakfast he decided to take a walk and get his bearings, after a short time the rain started falling as sleet and he returned to the hotel for what was a long and uncomfortable day.

The interpreter should have been in the hotel lobby at seven thirty but didn't arrive until nine. He was a young man of about eighteen and from his dress obviously a clerk. He introduced himself as Claude Maertens and without any apology or further conversation set off in the direction of the mine that loomed above the houses at the end of the main street. Trying to think the best of the situation he put it down to a mistake and followed.

After waiting half an hour in an outer office presided over by the French version of 'Cecil', they were called in to an office very similar to Maynard's. The Manager explained through Maertens that he would be giving them all possible assistance, but would not be able to do anything until the next day. In spite of his efforts to get someone to show him the job and the equipment, nothing could be done and they soon found themselves back out in the pit yard. Maertens said he would be back in the morning at seven thirty and left.

Another long day followed during which he speculated as to the whereabouts of Maertens being reasonably sure that he hadn't gone back to his normal work. The next days followed much the same pattern and it wasn't until Friday that he finally descended the mine, the French miner showing them the way was clearly displeased at being with him and Maertens looked frightened on what must have been his first underground visit.

It was a deeply depressing expedition. The description of the job's progress bore no relation to reality. He and Maynard had been lead to believe all that was needed was some engineering work in a prepared site. Instead, even transporting the pump to the site was going to be a major problem; the tunnel roof was very low and needed repairing before the large pump would pass through. The pump room site was unprepared and there was going to be a lot of pipework to make and install. Even if he got considerable help, there was at least three months work.

After a weekend spent killing time with long walks and visits to bars, Monday eventually came and some assistance did materialise. Progress was slow and frustrating, the assistance varied from day to day and the men supplied were clearly only the types no one else wanted. Steel girders ordered from the engineering workshop, had been sent to the wrong part of the workings and when they did eventually arrive they were not the size that he had asked for. He did not believe that the problems were due to incompetence, he had had plenty of time to scan a professional eye over the pit, and it seemed OK to him.

He suspected some of his instructions to workmen were being wrongly translated, but that wouldn't account for all his problems. At the end of the week, he knew there was no chance of success and something was going on that he didn't understand. He made up his mind to see Henri Masson and if more help weren't forthcoming, he would leave and suffer the consequences.

On Monday he went to the Lens address he had been given for Henri Masson. Waiting to be shown in to the office, he mentally rehearsed what to say, listing the problems he had encountered. However when he went in, encouraged by the friendly reception, instead he asked Masson outright what was going on.

Masson told him to sit down and then said "I have been expecting you; I am surprised it took so long! I think I owe you an apology for not telling you the full story earlier. I had better explain the background for you. I am only part owner of that mine, but I do own the royalties on the deep reserves to the West Side. They can only be worked when the water is under control. The rest of the mine is owned by a group of investors and a bank and they control the day-to-day working. If I can't get those deep coals opened I will be forced to sell out."

He continued "The Manager takes his orders from my partners and although he dare not openly refuse to help me, his loyalty is to them. When I couldn't get him to do the job, I called in engineers but they also needed assistance, when they didn't get it, they produced reports," he pointed to two bound folders on his desk. "When I discussed this with your Colonel Harrington his answer was to send someone to by-pass the locals. He is not a man for detail and he is used to giving orders and being obeyed." Looking embarrassed he confessed "I haven't been able to get mine obeyed  so I accepted his offer of help  and went along with him as a last resort. However  you need  proper help at the mine and as with the others before it does not look as though you will get it. Can you see any way forward?" he said.

Being spoken to on equal terms by a coal owner and asked for his opinion, was a new experience for him. Before Maynard, no senior manager had ever spoken to him and his only experience of financial intrigue had been how to delay paying his rent. In spite of all this and because the circumstances were so extraordinary, he felt able to suggest his own preferred solution to Masson. He thought for a few moments before he said "If I had my own men and paid them enough, we might be able to get moving but they would need to be outsiders." He knew enough about pit village politics to know that they would be marked men afterwards and "I would need another source of materials and an interpreter that I can trust."

Masson said " I had been trying to avoid doing it that way, it really is the last resort, you will get no help at all from the Manager and probably some obstruction. But you are right it's going to be the only way and you are also right about Maertens, he works for one of my partners." Looking at his watch, Masson surprised him again by inviting him to lunch. Lunch in the station restaurant was the best meal he had ever eaten and he drank wine for the first time in his life. There, and afterwards back at Masson's office, they worked out the details for the new approach.

On the train returning to Carvin he felt warm from the wine and good about the events of the morning. He had been resigned to an ignominious return home and unemployment, but now there was a chance of success. He was going to be provided with money for wages and materials. He had the address of a retired mine foreman in Douai who might find suitable men and take over the mining work and he had the name of an English speaking teacher in Carvin who might recommend a trustworthy interpreter. He had also decided that if he was to see the job through, he was going to have some more comfortable accommodation and added that to his list of things to do.

Later that evening, reasoning that a teacher would be home from work now, he walked the short distance to the address in what he surmised was the better end of town and furthest away from the pit. It was a two-storey house with shuttered windows and through the open gates in the high wall he could see a cobbled yard. He had the feeling it had seen better days. An old lady had answered the door but when he had spoken in English she had retreated and a moment later the teacher Thérèse Delmas appeared and asked him in. After he had explained his errand she took him into a cold front room that reminded him of his own less luxurious, but equally unused front room in Shirby.

Thérèse Delmas looked to be in her early thirties, had a slightly matronly appearance with severely tied back black hair that was starting to go grey. Dowdy dress and steel rimmed glasses didn't improve the overall impression. She looked exactly as he had expected, but she was not unfriendly and her English was too good to have been learnt at school. She told him that a young man to whom she had been giving lessons, might be interested in work, his grasp of the language should be good enough and she knew he needed the money.

After taking the young man's address he thanked her and prepared to leave, then as an afterthought asked if she knew a family he might lodge with. She thought for a moment and asking him to wait, left the room. He heard her talking in French to someone in the back of the house and presently she returned with a tall dark haired man who she introduced as Maurice, her husband. "We have a room at the back that used to be the maid's when our family still had one, would you like to see it?" she said.

The room was a single storey extension to the house off the cobbled yard and although a little musty, looked at least as comfortable as the hotel. On enquiring about meals he was told that Madame Delmas, Maurice's mother, was an excellent cook and that he could eat with them. It seemed the ideal solution and the price they agreed on would save him some money. He said yes, moved in the following morning, and then went to see the student Thérèse had recommended as an interpreter.

He immediately liked Jean, his English could have been better, but more important, he was friendly and seemed honest. Without giving too much away he satisfied himself that the youth didn't have any close connections with the colliery, such as relatives working there and probably could be trusted. A tall fair-haired lad of seventeen, he was going to study Electrical Engineering and was very enthusiastic at the prospect of earning some money before starting.

The following day Jean arrived early and they traveled to Douai to see Robert Gallini, the mine foreman Henri Masson had recommended. Gallini was a small man in his mid sixties but lean and fit looking for his age. It took some time to explain the nature of the job and although he tried to avoid discussing the politics, it was soon apparent that he had worked it out for himself. Gallini told him he would have to see the job before he could agree to get involved and they arranged to meet at the pit the next morning. He was a little disappointed and had hoped to get started recruiting immediately but on reflection decided he would have done the same given the chance.

Gallini said very little while they crawled around the

site next day, he made lots of notes and didn't give any sign of what he was thinking until they talked afterwards in a bar. After he had explained through Jean what mining work would be needed before they could start installing the pump, Paul realised just how much out of his depth he was. He was sure Gallini could be a valuable ally, he knew what he was doing and could be trusted. Offered twice the rate that Masson had suggested, he was clearly delighted and accepted.

Gallini moved with admirable speed; two days later he had assembled a dozen of the roughest looking men Paul had ever seen. It wasn't hard to see why they were available to start work immediately but Gallini assured him that they were all first class workers. At least, he reassured himself, they didn't look the sort who would take 'no for an answer' if anyone got in their way.

Now with some prospect of success, he wrote to Maynard and explained why he would not be back as arranged and now that the French were paying him, asked him to get his wages paid to Sarah. She hadn't replied to his letters, but he knew she would be running short of money soon and whatever the reason for her silence, there was little he could do about it until he returned.

When they started work in earnest the following week, things went better than he could have hoped. His rough team were under no illusion about their future prospects and didn't care who they upset. After some vicious altercations with the regular miners, the work progressed steadily. Lack of assistance from the pit manager was still causing delays, but he didn't think he was being actively obstructed.

Life with the Delmas family was comfortable and much less lonely than the weeks spent at the hotel. The old lady may have been a shrew, but she was a very good cook. Maurice was pleasant enough, but not speaking English, their relations were limited to smiles and gestures. Thérèse continued to be friendly and encouraged by her to borrow from her small library of books in English, for the first time read he most evenings before going to bed.

One evening after nearly two weeks with them, Thérèse asked him if he would like to join Maurice for a drink with friends at the hotel bar. The thought of an evening in the company of French speakers wasn't that appealing, but beginning to tire of reading every night, he agreed. In the lounge bar of the hotel he had been so glad to leave, Albert, a friend with whom Maurice worked at the town hall, joined them. The evening went well enough for a while, he made appropriate responses to jokes he didn't understand, and some communication was achieved by gestures.

The pair were obviously well known and exchanged greetings with most of the customers, some of whom lingered at their table for a time but none sat down or stayed very long. From his viewpoint facing out into the room over their shoulders, he was able to study the other customers, especially those who had been speaking to Maurice and Albert. What he saw gave him the feeling that the pair were not liked or maybe even feared by some. As they drank more, Maurice and Albert started to make what he guessed were crude suggestions to the waitress. She endured it with a fixed smile and artificial jollity but as she turned away from their table he could see her face in the mirror behind the bar, it had a look of contempt.

He had had enough of it and was about to leave when he saw something which intrigued him, at the window a boy about fourteen was looking in and he was almost sure that something passed between him and Maurice, just a look and then he was gone. The one benefit of not speaking the language was the ease, at which he was able to overcome objections to his leaving early, he motioned tiredness and left.

It was a fine evening and still light, so instead of returning to his room he decided to investigate the fishing potential of the canal. It was a pleasant walk but as the light failed, not wanting to fall in, he left the towpath at the next bridge and followed the railway line back to the town.

Walking along the track was getting harder as it became darker and he was glad to see the town lights ahead. Close to where the railway crossed the road he saw light coming from a shed that was probably a railway workers store and then heard a man sniggering. He knew which man; it was Albert, it had been partly due to that he had left the bar early. The light either from a candle or hurricane lamp showed through the window and his curiosity got the better of him. The window was almost opaque with dirt but there was no mistaking what he saw. Maurice had the boy he had seen earlier at the bar window, against a wall kissing him and his hand was inside the boy's trousers; Albert stood close by leering. For reasons he couldn't explain, he ran and only slowed down when he tripped on a sleeper.

Back in his room, he felt disgusted and ashamed. Not knowing why he should feel responsible, he tried to think what he should do. His first reaction had been to confront him and then leave but eventually told himself that it was none of his business and nobody seemed to be forcing the boy. He knew that he was only justifying his own self-interest, these were comfortable lodgings, he didn't want to leave and felt ashamed of himself.

He had worried about how he would feel meeting Maurice and sitting at the same table, but in the event it wasn't difficult. He seemed to be back to his old pleasant self and Paul hid behind the language barrier, almost like a wall. He wasn't invited to the bar again and was glad not to have to refuse. It was about this time that he noticed Thérèse wince as if in pain getting up from the table and later when she reached to take a plate off a high shelf her cuffs rode up a little and he thought he saw a bruise on her arm.

The days settled into a comfortable routine. Gallini had charge of the mining work and most days there was little for Paul to do, leaving him free to concentrate on the engineering work.

When he had done what he could in advance, he and Jean were able to spend less time at the mine and with

Jean acting as guide, they did a little sightseeing and spent some of Masson's money on lunches while they were out.

# CHAPTER 3

## THÉRÈSE

After the incident with the boy, Paul kept pretty much to himself, rarely entering the house except for meals, made a point of being punctual and not hanging around afterwards.

Wednesday evening the following week, bored with the book he was reading, he decided to try something else from the collection. Since Thérèse had told him not to keep asking for permission, he went across to the house and walked in without knocking. The family were usually at a church function on Wednesdays, but when he opened the kitchen door he found Thérèse was there. She was just about to get into a tin bath in front of the fire, she turned round and looked at him for a moment before reaching for a towel. She didn't speak and gave him a look that was neither hostile nor surprised. Burning with embarrassment, he muttered apologies and fled.

The whole incident hadn't lasted more than a few seconds but as he sat in his room afterwards, every detail was quite clear and still embarrassed him. Without the dowdy clothes and spectacles, with her hair down, she was an attractive woman. He hadn't seen anyone but Sarah naked before and even that was a rare event, in spite of himself he found himself comparing them. Thérèse was a little plumper but he found it hard to get what he had seen out of his mind.

Something else bothered him though; he was almost certain that she had deliberately hesitated before covering herself and in that moment he had seen bruises on her ribs and a circular bruise on her left breast that could only be from a bite. He already suspected it and now he was sure, that bastard was beating his wife. Wife beating wasn't uncommon in Shirby, usually the result of drink, but since he had never seen him drunk there wasn't even that excuse.
He decided to spend even less time with the Delmas family after this, Thérèse never mentioned it but occasional looks from her reminded him, if there was any chance of forgetting, that they had a secret and she seemed glad to share it.

It was Masson's clerk who told him that the following Monday was a religious holiday and with his workforce 'worshipping' in bars he might as well take the day off too. He decided on a days fishing, Thérèse had told him he could borrow fishing tackle that had belonged to her late father in law. He had invited Jean along but when he had refused he suspected the lad had more interesting plans that probably included the girl he had seen him with occasionally.

Taking advantage of the cool morning air, he left before the Delmas, who were going to visit family in Lille, were up. He chose a spot along the towpath well away from the town and it fished quite well for a time, but as it got warmer the fish retreated and he relaxed in the sunshine, not expecting to catch much more. About to pack up and go to a bar for some lunch, he was surprised to see Thérèse coming along the path on a bicycle. Stopping, she said "I have got some lunch here" pointing to the basket on the front of the bicycle "If you like we could share it." He knew it was no accidental meeting, she must have cycled quite a long way to find him, and he wondered why. She sat beside him and, after watching him release the three Perch he had caught, said " Let's eat!"

They moved off the towpath into the field behind and into the shade of a tree. There was bread, cheese, cold chicken and a bottle of wine; while they ate she told him how she had feigned illness to avoid the trip to Lille. She disliked Maurice's relatives, describing them as pious hypocrites who lived for family feuds. When she impersonated them he discovered just how funny she could be. On neutral ground without her husband or mother in law around, he felt much more relaxed with her. She told him how she had spent ten years as a child in Broadstairs where her father had been a working as a chef. He told her of childhood spent in a succession of towns and villages just like this one. They talked for a long time but as if by agreement both ended their previous lives before marriage.

He never really knew who made the first move but when they found themselves kissing neither of them tried to stop. He reached inside her blouse and cupped her breast. She flinched and caught his hand, bringing back memories of teenage fumbling with girls who permitted certain liberties before calling a halt. Those thoughts were instantly forgotten when she kept hold of his hand and put it under her skirt onto her thigh, he was still expecting a halt to be called until he found that she wasn't wearing knickers. He broke off kissing her and saw with her eyes starting to fill with tears, what it must have cost her to do this.

She seemed to come to a decision; stood up straightened her clothes and said, "I don't think I want to do this" and then in a much quieter voice "In a field." He watched her ride away wondering what to do. He had never been unfaithful to Sarah but if she hadn't stopped, they would have made love there and then. If he followed her to the house there would be no heat of the moment excuse, but he did anyway.

As he walked back, he thought about Sarah, he didn't love her and she didn't love him but she was his wife, Thérèse was married to a man who preferred boys and ill-treated her, but still she was a married woman, there was no future in it.

When he entered his room and found her waiting, he knew there was not going to be any discussion. Neither them of them speaking, he tried to help her undress as calmly as he could with shaking hands, but she couldn't wait and took over. When they were both naked she began moving backwards until they fell in a heap on the bed. It wasn't easy to enter her and realising it was hurting her he tried to pull back but she held him tightly to her. He was trying not to hurt her and was glad it was soon over but she still didn't want to let him go. They lay for a time without speaking and she cried gently, wetting his shoulder. When the silence became too much he said "You haven't done this before" and she nodded. He didn't know why, but it seemed to make a lot of difference and he felt very touched by it.

With the last reserve between them gone, her story flooded out. Maurice was five years her senior, they had married four years ago when he left the Army. There had been other men interested, but on learning she had been told while quite young that she wouldn't have children, none of them had stayed around. At twenty-eight when she had given up hope of marriage, Maurice proposed. Children didn't bother him, he needed a wife. Maurice has ambitions and being seen for a 'mother's boy' would not help him achieve them. She didn't want the life of a spinster and closed her eyes to it, telling herself that she could change him "And he never made love to you" he asked "He tried at first but couldn't manage it and when I found out about the boys, I wouldn't let him try after that" she said. "Has he ever tried to..." He hesitated, embarrassed to use the words he knew for sodomy. "Yes now and again" she said, not waiting for him to finish "but I threaten to tell his mother and that stops him, then he hits me instead" she looked down to her bruised breast.

Thinking back to the reactions of the people in the bar that night, he asked "Why are people afraid of him?" To answer this she explained how power and influence worked in the town, the church and the ruling party, socialist in this case and of course the Town Hall administration. Maurice had a foothold in all of them, "People who cross him usually regret it" she said. He recognised the set-up perfectly, if she had substituted Chapel for Catholic Church she may as well have described Shirby and he could even put a name to its own 'Maurice'.

"Tell me about your wife now" she said. Even though he was in bed with another woman it seemed disloyal to criticise Sarah and he had to think hard about his marriage before answering. "I am a disappointment to her, I have stopped caring, and we don't love each other enough to do anything about it." It came as a surprise hearing himself say it; it was the first time he had really put into words what was wrong.

The conversation seemed to send them both off into private thought for a time, until she said, "They will be back before long, but we could have time to" she didn't finish but put his hand back between her legs. It lasted much longer and she was obviously sore but it didn't stop her encouraging him. When it was over she got out of bed and dressed quickly. "You are a lovely man Paul" she said and kissed him briefly. Turning as she went towards the door she said shyly "It won't hurt next time, so I am told" and then with a giggle "but I don't think I will be riding my bicycle just yet." He had been feeling serious and emotional, but couldn't help laughing as well.

If Maurice had had the slightest interest in his wife,

they would have been found out in days. His mother, Sylvine didn't miss glances and accidental touching but he seemed totally oblivious to it. Try as she may Thérèse couldn't get out of accompanying him to church and his Wednesday committee and they were unable be alone again that week. It seemed the following week was going to be the same but on Tuesday evening she could barely contain herself when she got him alone for a moment. A letter had arrived for Maurice from the Army, his annual recall to the reserve had been moved forward and he had been told to report for a two-week training camp next week. They would have two whole weeks alone, Sylvine would, as always, visit her sister. She never stayed to do any cooking or housework if her son was not going to benefit. In spite of this they still took risks, touching and kissing that week.

When Maurice, in his sergeants uniform left on Sunday afternoon Paul was relieved they had not been exposed. Sylvine wasn't fooled, but she wasn't going to tell Maurice. A web of secrets and pretence held the Delmas family together, she knew about Maurice's vice and always had but he was unaware of that and more than anything, feared her finding out. Sylvine would not expose them because it would almost certainly lead to a scandal that couldn't be contained in the family. Maurice's vice was fairly well known but Thérèse couldn't admit to knowing unless she left him and she had nowhere to go. She explained all this when it became clear from Sylvine's looks at him that she knew.

None of this mattered now. Sylvine was scarcely out

of the house before they were pulling each other's clothes off. There was no time for care with buttons or removing layers this time, they had both thought of little else since the last time.

The next two weeks were the happiest either of them had spent in their lives. They made love as often as they could, so often that her bicycle joke came out again and again. She may have been a thirty two year old virgin when it started but she was an enthusiastic learner. Before long, she was totally uninhibited and made him wonder how he had ever lived without this woman or would be able to when it was over. They slept crushed up together in a single bed in his room; it was their way of putting distance between what they had and the Delmas family home. When he got back from work, Thérèse home before him, had a stove full of hot water, ready for his bath. When he got in she helped him bathe. When they couldn't wait for him to bathe, she would get covered in coal dust too and they would have to bathe each other.

Much as they tried, the prospect of Maurice's return hung over the last few days like a cloud. He was due back around noon on Saturday, as their own act of defiance they made love on the kitchen floor almost up to the point his footsteps were heard in the yard.

He kept his distance from the Delmas that weekend; but Maurice was so full of himself and his achievements, he had been put forward for promotion to Sergeant Major, he scarcely noticed him. Sylvine continued the campaign of silent suspicion towards them but otherwise life returned to normal.

An event took place on the 28th of June that was going to make life anything but normal, but nobody in the Delmas household heard until later that week and then didn't think it was of any significance. The Archduke Franz Ferdinand of Austria had been shot in Sarajevo. Paul had heard of neither the Duke nor Sarajevo and forgot about it almost as soon as Thérèse had finished telling him. He had more mundane problems; the work was beginning to be held up waiting for materials to be paid for. The local merchants would not extend credit to his unorthodox operation; it was strictly cash on delivery.

He made an appointment to see Henri Masson on Thursday and went to discuss it with him. He suggested that the clerk came over more often but Masson decided that it would be more efficient to place money into an account at the Amiens Mutual Bank in Lens and give him authority to draw on it. This responsibility worried him but Masson was adamant, as he also was, that he would need properly kept books and receipts for all expenditure. He had never kept books and asked Thérèse's advice that evening. Her face lit up "Let me do it and if you offer to pay me a small wage Maurice will be all for it. It s just the excuse we need to be alone together."

The following week, accompanied by Jean, he presented his letter of authority to the bank and had no further problems obtaining cash. On their first bookkeeping evening, to suspicious looks from Sylvine and indifference from Maurice, they took his papers into the front room where they then took an enormous risk. Thérèse whispered "I have something for you, if you can do it quietly" and put his hand between her thighs. Sitting on the edge of the table, biting her lip to keep quiet, she looked over his shoulders at the door separating them from Maurice and his mother who were playing the piano in the next room.

Rumours of war began to dominate conversation everywhere but he and Thérèse were oblivious to it, they just schemed to grab occasional moments together. A week after the bookkeeping incident it was Bastille Day. The Delmas family were going as usual to the dismal family gathering in Lille, Thérèse feigned illness so convincingly that Sylvine briefly considered staying at home with her, before eventually advising her to stay in bed instead. Just this once she obeyed her and almost ran to Paul's bed as they left.

He knew they couldn't put off any longer talking about the future, pressing his face hard into her breasts and turning just enough to speak he said "This is how I want to die." Thérèse told him what he wanted to hear when she said "But only when you are a very old man." Deciding to leave Sarah had taken weeks of agonising; it took her not a moment to make her decision.

They talked inconclusively of where they might go. She had a cousin, a farmer in Belgium, who had room and could possibly provide work, but she didn't know the kind of reception she would get turning up with a lover, especially one who spoke no French. He knew that work could be found in the new Kent coalfield, it was so short of men that they would accept anybody but they had no money and the question of Sarah still remained.

Talk of war now became so persistent that they couldn't ignore it any longer and he had to consider his own situation. He had no idea if it would affect Britain but his position here looked certain to change. When on the 2nd of August the Army was mobilised and Maurice received his orders to report for duty, the decision couldn't be delayed any longer .

Next morning he went to seek advice from Masson, but he wasn't there, he too had been recalled to his regiment, but he had left a letter for him. It told him to wind the job up right away, go home and to ignore the wild French talk of invading Germany. He said he hoped he was wrong but thought it more likely that they would have German troops in Carvin before the month was out . He also said that he had written to Colonel Harrington thanking him for the excellent assistance he had provided and hoped it could be sorted out after the war. He recognised the kindness of that act and was grateful for the help it was trying to offer.

In spite of the urgency, he took his time stopping the work, some of the men had already gone to the Army, and on Wednesday he paid off those who remained. Reluctantly he allowed them to take him drinking and felt quite touched by their rough friendship and the gratitude for a few weeks work. That evening while he recovered from the drink, Thérèse made the final entries in the account book, with the men paid and suppliers bills met there remained 9890 Francs in the account.

With Maurice gone, ignoring Sylvine's presence they were openly living together determined to make the most of the time remaining. This was too much for Sylvine and after she was reminded of the consequences for her son if they were betrayed, she moved out.

# CHAPTER 4

## UNWELCOME NEWS

Paul and Thérèse didn't attract any attention when they parted at Lens station on the 9th of August. Scores of couples were parting and they were all thinking of their own uncertain futures.

The only decision they had been able to make was for him to return home; break with Sarah, find work away from Shirby, raise some money, send for her or come back. They had no idea how long it would take or what affect the war might have. Jean stood back not wanting to intrude, but as Paul was about to get on the train he embraced him and promised to do anything he could for both of them.

If the journey out had seemed difficult, the return was a nightmare. The French Army had requisitioned most trains and with thousands on the move it had taken five days to get back. The delays at each change had been so long, he thought it quite possible that he could have walked to Boulogne quicker. Boulogne had been full of British troops of the expeditionary force and even after bribing a ticket clerk with most of his remaining cash, it took two days to get on a ferry.

When he finally arrived home he was filthy and exhausted. He didn't look or feel like a returning hero and Sarah wasn't hanging out welcome flags either. One look at Sarah's thickening waist warned him what was coming next and it was very unwelcome news.

"I am so glad you could drag yourself away from your new friends, look what you have done to me" she said pointing to her waist. The tirade continued in the same vein until she had exhausted herself and retreated with tears and slammed doors to the bedroom. Sarah didn't usually resort to shouting and it was clear she had been rehearsing this ever since she had found out. There was no reasoning with her, no responsibility for her own part in the act and no explanation why she hadn't written to tell him.

Deserting the child was out of the question, he would have to abandon Thérèse and be tied to Sarah. He had wanted a child before their marriage went sour, now he was going to be its prisoner. He considered waiting until the child was born before telling Thérèse in case the pregnancy failed but felt ashamed of dark thoughts that even welcomed the idea as a solution.

Eventually after days of indecision, he wrote. The letter had been written and rewritten so many times when he finally posted it he couldn't be sure exactly what it had said other than a statement of the facts, asking for forgiveness and expressions of love. Two days later, a policeman at his door handed him the letter back; it had been opened. With a smirk on his face, the policeman warned him consequences, should he write again to an address in a war zone. It was fortunate that Sarah, who had practically moved in at her mothers wasn't there; his private problems were bad enough without fuelling the fire.

After a days' rest, he had been to see Maynard to find out if he still had a job, after the way the project had ended. His reception at the pit was better than expected, he wasn't kept waiting long in Cecil's office before Maynard had shouted "Come in Belcher" and "Cecil get us some tea!" Inside, Maynard said, "Sit down and tell me the whole story." When he had finished, Maynard said, "What do you think you actually achieved there?" He had the future to think about now and decided honesty would serve him best. "Not very much Mr. Maynard, the pump is still in a packing crate and the job's stopped." "Bollocks!" exclaimed Maynard "You did well to survive and get the job moving at all. Masson was impressed and Harrington regards it as a personal triumph would you believe! We would have been in the shit if you had made a balls of things, you know that don't you!" He noticed the use of 'we' and agreed. As he was leaving Maynard said "Thanks Belcher, I will have a word with Joe about you."

He got the impression that Joe didn't enjoy having a protégé of the Manager in his department but his fortunes did begin to improve. It wasn't dramatic, but he began to be put in charge of jobs on which he had previously only been a participant and wasn't sent to do a pump man's shift again.

Maynard, whilst not openly friendly, did acknowledge him with a nod when their paths occasionally crossed. The most notable incident was not at the pit but Chesterfield market. With the baby's arrival imminent, he and Sarah, who had barely been speaking, called a truce and went shopping for baby things. Maynard, accompanied by his wife, stopped them in street, raised his hat to Sarah and congratulated them on the 'forthcoming event', Mrs. Maynard had seemed very kind and he thought it was only a look from Maynard that prevented her reaching for her purse. Sarah could hardly have been more pleased if it had been royalty. In her mind the foreign assignment once again became the start of their advancement and she almost forgot the part that it had played in her present condition.

When Dorothy was born on the 14th of December Sarah seemed very happy and he was overjoyed but it did not bring them any closer together. Sarah was a good mother, Dorothy was loved, well dressed and cared for but she was determined there would be no more children. This suited them both and her refusal to sleep with him saved him from having to explain why he didn't want her. He still didn't want to think about the future without Thérèse but Dorothy filled every other space in his life.

Maynard's only son was an officer in the Sherwood Foresters. Paul had been unaware of his existence until his photograph appeared in the Mansfield Echo, reported as missing at Loos. The effect on Maynard was dramatic, when he saw him shortly afterwards, he looked a broken man, and it surprised no one when he had a stroke in November 1915 and he didn't return to work.

The manager who replaced him was no worse than any other but Paul meant nothing to him and when he had to spend a shift as a pump man again, he knew it.

# CHAPTER 5

## THE WAR AND COAL

In March 1916 Paul decided, to visit Maynard, even if only once. Sarah couldn't see any point to it since they had hardly been friends, but now that that they had ceased, he could see that there had been interventions on his behalf and he was grateful.

The Maynard's house was at the end of a terrace of large villa type houses on Mansfield Road. He called first and checked with Mrs. Maynard that he was well enough for visitors and arranged to come back on Saturday afternoon. Maynard; apart from a slight slur and some difficulty walking had recovered well, they sat drinking tea in his study for about half an hour, but finding it hard to make conversation he regretted coming. They didn't have much in common apart from the French episode and the mining industry and that had been at vastly different levels. It became easier however when he discovered their shared interest in fishing. Leaving as soon as seemed respectable, Maynard made no attempt to stop him; and he didn't think he should come again.

Mrs. Maynard, on the pretext of showing him out, waylaid him and took him into the front parlour, "You will come again Paul, please" she said. "Do you really think he wants to see me?" he replied. "You are the first visitor he has had other than old women and he has been so looking forward to it" she continued, "he finds it hard to talk, always has but don't be put off by that. Now before you go, tell me about the baby, was it a boy or a girl?" When he did leave he had been forced by her to accept a silver mug for the baby, promise to bring Dorothy along next time and agree to call her Alice in future.

About this time, he received the first letter from Jean, he had been called up into the Army and expected to serve at the front quite soon. Henri Masson was dead, he had been killed at Longwy when the war was only two weeks old. He was sorry to hear this; Masson had been kind to him, when he didn't have to be. The final piece of news was about Thérèse, Jean carefully worded it, correctly assuming Sarah would see it. He talked about the whole Delmas family as though they had all been his friends, that Madame Delmas had been able to leave before the Germans arrived but had no further details or an address. It was a relief to know she was thought to be alive and out of danger but it didn't ease the pain he still felt about her.

The visits to Maynard continued, sometimes he took Dorothy and Alice would play with her while he sat with Maynard and other times when Maynard was tired he sat with Alice in the parlour. The visits to Maynard were a sort of duty but Alice had become a friend, she was broadminded and kind with a sense of humour that sometimes had him blushing. He would drink tea with Maynard but when he joined her in the parlour they drank whisky. The Maynards had travelled a lot and he was fascinated with her accounts of her youth in India and East Africa. Maynard never mentioned his son but Alice would talk about him even though it usually ended in tears.

In September he received a letter from Jean that was a mixture of good and bad news. He was in hospital and was recovering from a wound received in June at Verdun. He had lost part of his right foot but at least he was going to live and would not be going back to war. That there could be any bright side to losing a foot made him wonder just how bad the front must have been. There was no further word about Thérèse and he didn't expect any now until the war ended and there was no sign of that.

The community in Shirby was less affected by the carnage than most. Miners being in a reserved occupation were going to have to stay at home whether they liked it or not and some of those who had rushed to enlist in the first months had even been brought back from the trenches. In spite of this they were still short of men to produce enough coal for the war effort. Working long hours of overtime, he spent little time at home with Sarah and it suited them both, but life had settled into a reasonable 'peace' centered on Dorothy.

By Christmas 1917 relations between them had improved, Dorothy was old enough to enjoy it now and they worked together to make it special for her. With the overtime and higher wages, for once money was not quite such a problem. Sarah queued endlessly to get extra food and luxuries; and together they gathered holly and made decorations. Alice gave them a luxury food hamper and for Dorothy there was an expensive looking rocking horse that had been her son's. Dorothy loved it.

It was probably the happiest day of their marriage, for the first time they felt like a family. After Dorothy had gone to bed they sat by the fire, ate nuts and opened the bottle of Port from the hamper. The Port and the good feeling of the day touched Sarah and presently she said "It's been so nice today let's see if we can keep it up, lets go to bed" seeing him looking undecided, she said "Please." It was the best moment yet between them, they made love and for one of the few times since France he didn't think about Thérèse.

Their relations remained good in the months that followed; they avoided confrontations and began to enjoy each other's company more. They both knew that they were making the best of a marriage they shouldn't be in, but once they stopped trying to change each other, they were happier. He still wanted Thérèse but wouldn't leave Dorothy for her and began to think that if he could get Sarah away from her family's influence, there might be a chance for them.

In early June the Mansfield Echo began advertising vacancies at Betteshanger Colliery, in Kent and there was housing with the jobs. Agents for the company were interviewing at a public house in Mansfield each Wednesday. Without telling Sarah, he decided to go along the following week. The interview went very well, he had been willing to accept anything similar to his present job, but the agent had been very interested in the French episode and told him they were short of men with supervisory experience. He said that the French job proved he could show initiative and providing he backed the story up with a reference from Maynard, he would very likely be offered a foreman's position.

Sarah thought it was a wonderful idea and the following day went to tell her parents the good news. When she returned she was equally enthusiastic but for a different plan. "My father said after the war he should be able get you a job at the railway works in Derby instead and he might even be able to get us a railway cottage near them. That would be better than going all that way to Kent don't you think?"

He could not think of anything worse than being in debt to her father or living near her mother. Neither of them were in a mood for compromise and after hurtful words between them, they agreed to abandon both plans.

The response from her family convinced him that he had been right and he didn't give up the idea altogether. He would wait and see what happened after the war, which couldn't be long now, before trying again. There were bound to be changes when all the troops came back, but it was hard to tell how they would be affected.

Through 1918 he studied the progress of the war with more interest, after looking as though it was lost in the spring, through the summer and autumn the tide had definitely turned. The papers still filled pages with casualty lists, but the maps printed for 'armchair warriors' were starting to show the front moving back towards Germany.

In September, all around people were ill and many had already died. When he woke in the night feeling very hot, he found Sarah was drenched with sweat. Almost moaning when she said "I feel so bad," they both knew it was the flu. She had a miserable time for the next two weeks and hadn't fully recovered when he fell ill himself. He and neighbours had managed to mind Dorothy and look after Sarah but now he was ill, her mother came and took charge. Too ill to care at first it wasn't until he began to feel better he saw the poisonous effect she had on Sarah. He wasn't surprised when an affectionate touch was brushed off but he was surprised to feel hurt.

That hurt was soon forgotten when Dorothy fell ill and after only a week, died on October the 4th. Sarah had never found it easy to show Dorothy affection, but it was not because she loved her any less and was inconsolable. They grieved separately and had nothing for each other. At the graveside he held Alice, Sarah had retreated somewhere and stood dry eyed.

It was some weeks after the funeral before he saw Alice again. Without any warning she asked, "What's wrong between you and Sarah?" He had never discussed his marriage problems with her and didn't know how to start, so he said "Things will be OK when get we over this" but she said "I don't believe that and neither do you, why did you cry on my shoulder and not hers?" Without waiting for an answer she went to the drinks cabinet and brought back a bottle of whiskey and two tumblers.

She had become his closest friend and the only person he could trust, desperate to talk to someone, he told her the whole story including Thérèse's part, Alice just listened. He hadn't expected criticism and wasn't ready for her response. "How long do you intend making yourself and Sarah unhappy, the next forty years?" she had never spoken to him sharply before and he was shocked. "Where is Thérèse now?" "I don't know, I had word she got away before the Germans came but have heard no more and don't have an address, she could even be dead for all I know." Alice said "Even if she is, you are no use to Sarah and she won't make you happy either."

She silenced him before he could say any more and said, "I know what I am talking about. Maynard isn't really my name, it's Henderson, and Henderson is my husbands name." He said, "You and Mr. Maynard aren't married!" "No I am still married to Richard Arthur Henderson, that's if he is still alive. The last time I saw him was in Wankie, that's in Matabeleland, in 1891. March the 3rd was the day I walked out on him; he was too drunk to notice me go. Maynard and I got a train to Beira and the next ship to England." He was about to ask why and then realised she was going to tell him. "I loved Maynard and I didn't love my husband, we had been married 8 years, he wasn't cruel but he preferred the bottle and his cronies at the club, to me. I don't even think he was unfaithful and that was unusual there I can tell you! Maynard was working at the colliery there; we met at the club and a fortnight later we ran away together."

He was amazed to think of that taciturn man in the next room, acting that way. She continued "I told you my father was in the Colonial Service, after I left school I went back to Africa and we moved around a lot, I thought it was a good life then. I married the first man who asked me and, had I accepted the gin and bridge party existence with the occasional lover like the other wives, I would still be there.

I had a beautiful house with servants for everything. Instead I have lived in villages and towns like this ever since, Scotland, Durham, Wales and here and never regretted it for a moment." She paused and he thought she might cry but she carried on "Every few years the rumours would catch up with us, some spiteful owner's wife would hear and we had to move on. Maynard sometimes had to go back to being an Undermanager and even Overman once but he never cared. We had our son and we had each other, that's all we needed. You don't know Maynard, not many people do, he hasn't got any friends, and he never wanted any, just me. But now he can't work he does miss talking to men occasionally, that's why he likes to see you."

"That's me; now back to Thérèse, now you haven't got little Dorothy what's stopping you from trying to find her now the war is over, worry about how you are going to live afterwards."

He felt quite drunk when he left, he had been there three hours, and they had finished the bottle. He had started to see Alice as a mother figure but after this he felt quite differently towards her.

# CHAPTER 6

## POOR RELATIONS

It had been three weeks and worryingly Thérèse had still had no word from Paul, but even more worrying was the arrival in Carvin of Belgian refugees fleeing the Germans. Maurice had predicted a war of glorious victories and rapid defeat of Germany but it was turning out very different.

Thoughts of Paul's return and a new life together were replaced with more urgent considerations. If she and Sylvine didn't also flee, the war, however long it lasted, was going to be spent under German occupation. On her way home from the school had seen yet another group of bedraggled refugees arrive and deciding it couldn't be put off any longer, said to Sylvine "We have to leave and we can't go to my cousin in Belgium, so do you know anyone far enough away from here who would take us in?" Answering with more confidence than she actually felt she said "I am sure Monsieur Delmas's cousins in Dijon would be happy to see us, they were always very fond of Louis." Thérèse had never met them and hadn't known her to visit them either, but with no other option she agreed.

When they packed, they had not known how much walking there would be and it wasn't long before they had to abandon most of their belongings, just keeping what they could carry. After a week of interminable delays, spells of walking when trains failed to arrive, and sleeping in waiting rooms and churches they were exhausted and still less than half way. When in Soissons they finally found a hotel willing to take them, Sylvine was incapable of going any further and she was feeling very unwell herself.

After two days rest, Sylvine feeling recovered wanted to leave but Thérèse was forced to admit that still feeling unwell she couldn't and they stayed a third. Rested, both feeling a little better they moved on and with two trains they reached Troyes in a day. At the station and by now in pain and bleeding she had no option but to confide in Sylvine who amazed her by saying "I think you might be pregnant?" then not in an unkind way she added "You have certainly done enough to bring it about." She had never considered the possibility and having missed all the usual signs it came as shock to realise that she was probably right. Sylvine went on "I have had my problems and know enough to see that if you don't get rest and help you will lose it" then in what sounded like a question she said "Although its obviously not Maurice's we don't want that to happen do we?" Thérèse just nodded.

They found a seat in the buffet and while Sylvine went for help she tried to think what could be done.

She was torn between delight at carrying Paul's child, and worry bordering on panic knowing it couldn't be kept from Maurice. The crowds, noise and tobacco smoke in the buffet were more than she could bear but just as she was thinking of going outside Sylvine returned. Pointing to a bar across the road she said "We can have a room above there, there is no chance of a doctor but the bar owner knows a nurse who will come."

The help was in vain and during the night the baby was lost. Thérèse didn't know how she would have managed without Sylvine or how much it must have cost and not only in money but it wasn't to be a new beginning between them. Before long, relations between them returned to normal and strangely she found this 'old' Sylvine easier to cope with than the kinder person she had glimpsed.

Later, thinking what had could have bought about the sudden change she wondered if she had too suffered in a similar way with her own husband and marriage but they never discussed it and she would never know.

The Fiske family lived on the outskirts of Dijon and Madame Fiske was a cousin of Sylvine's late husband. They had not seen each other for years, greetings were just about polite, and it was obvious their unannounced arrival was hardly welcome. They certainly had room to spare, the house was much larger than the Delmas home in Carvin but when showing them to their room Madame Fisk pointedly said, "This is all we can offer but it should do until you find somewhere else."

Monsieur Fiske disappeared each day to the fabric and drapery store he owned in nearby Quetigny, taking his eighteen-year-old daughter Eloise with him. Eloise looked unhappy with the arrangement and when Thérèse went shopping for materials to replace her lost clothing, it was clear why. Trade was poor, there was little enough for even one to do, and this probably explained both Eloise's attitude and the parsimony of Madame Fiske.

When they had arrived there had been a cook and a part time maid, but it wasn't long before Sylvine, apparently willingly, took over in the kitchen and the cook disappeared. Sylvine had some money and they had been paying guests but their willingness to assist around the house soon began to place them into a 'poor relation' role. What had been requests, particularly to Thérèse, started to become more like instructions. When the maid left it was said to be for well-paid war work but she suspected she had been sacked in favour of unpaid help from herself.

After some weeks and with their visit starting to look more long term, Eloise began trying to treat Thérèse as a servant. Being asked by her to fetch a book from her room or pick up her laundry, convinced her that it was time to look for work outside the Fiske home. Sylvine was happy as a cook but she wasn't going to skivvy for her keep, or take orders from a sulky teenager for the rest of a war with no end in sight.

The opportunity came much sooner than she had

expected, whilst shopping in the village she learned from the grocer that the school had just lost yet another teacher to the army and was finding it difficult to cope. She went to the school immediately and at the end of a short interview with the head teacher, his final question was "When can you start?"

The arrival in the Fiske household of a new 'maid of all work' shortly afterwards confirmed what Thérèse had suspected about the departure of her predecessor. She enjoyed her work; liked her colleagues and with less time spent at the Fiske's, life settled into a dull but comfortable routine and for the first time in years, she was safe from Maurice.

Paul had no way of contacting her, she had written to Jean with her new address but as he hadn't replied she could only assume he never received it. Not daring to write to his home there seemed little to be done but wait and as the weeks turned into months it did get easier.

The war was in its third year when Maurice was given an administrative position in the rear of the fighting and now seemed likely to survive. Fearing, Paul might have found it too hard to leave Sarah and come back for her, she now urgently looked at what options that didn't include Maurice were open to her. Life would be difficult on what she currently earned but with just a little more, paying her own way and independence seemed possible. This dream came a little closer with a rise in pay when, following the departure for the war of yet another teacher, she was made head of the junior school.

Having almost given up hope of Paul returning and feeling lonely, when Emile, a teacher in the boys school began to show interest in her it was not unwelcome. Alone after an evening event at the school he somewhat awkwardly kissed her, she didn't resist but they were soon interrupted by the caretaker doing his rounds. He was nice young man who had been gassed and invalided out of the army, he was funny, and they had a lot of interests in common.

Already having crossed the 'adultery line' she told herself an affair with a single man wouldn't harm anybody but she did worry whether he was worldly enough to avoid getting her pregnant. Lack of opportunity and privacy held them back and when, it had gone no further than kisses, he was moved to another school, it was a relief the decision had been made for her.

The end of the war was a mixed blessing for Thérèse; glad like everyone the destruction and killing had ended but as she had feared, Maurice had not only survived but using political influence, had been quickly demobilised. The former head of the junior school had also come through unscathed and as a result she lost her position and with it for the moment at least, the dream of independence.

She was not sorry to leave the Fiskes, after nearly four years they were still never going to be friends, but it had been a refuge. She had not given up hope of a new life; with Paul or more likely independence, however for the moment she couldn't see a way out of returning to Carvin and that meant Maurice.

Back in the battered and much changed town, Maurice treating the war as just a temporary delay in achieving his ambitions, took up his old life and ways. Their vandalised home was more or less habitable and the teaching post that had awaited her meant she least escaped the house during the day.

However, he hadn't changed, but it wasn't until her 'protector' Sylvine died and the cruelty became very much worse, that in desperation she wrote to Paul.

# CHAPTER 7

## A FRESH START

Paul had known when they lost Dorothy that they had also lost any chance of happiness or reason to stay together. He couldn't stop thinking about Alice's advice to make a fresh start and look for Thérèse but it wasn't until after Christmas he acted. With relations between them at a new low after they had been forced to spend extra time together, he wrote to Jean asking if he knew where she was.

It was early February before he got a reply and it was fortunate that Sarah didn't see it. Jean had abandoned the caution of his previous letters and wrote;

*Dear Friend*
*I am just back from Carvin, The Germans kept the mines working through the occupation and the main battles missed it so although there is much destruction it is not as badly damaged as some. Most of the damage there is was done deliberately before they left. The mine is ruined and most of the buildings are damaged in some way but people are moving back quite quickly.*

*I have serious news for you, Maurice is back, he is strutting about wearing a medal and it seems certain he will be Mayor after the elections in April . Thérèse I have not seen myself but my sister has and Thérèse had a black eye. Madame Sylvine is ill and might even be dead before you get this. Can you help her?*

*I have heard a foul story about Delmas from an old school friend just returned from captivity in Germany. He was serving under him at Verdun and has sworn that he saw Delmas shoot one of his superior officers who had attempted to stop him deserting, not only that, but by bringing in the officers body he gained a bravery award. My friend never reported it and soon after was taken prisoner, he is ill and may not live but he has written it all down and I have the original, maybe you could use it against him.*

*Your friend Jean*

He wrote straight away to Thérèse and sent it to Jean, asking him to get it to her without Maurice finding out.

*Thérèse*
*Leave him as soon as you can and go to Boulogne. I will meet you there; I know where I can get a job and somewhere to live. Write and tell me where to meet you. I will just need a few days to come. If he tries to stop you, tell him your friends have been speaking to a member of his regiment who saw what he did to get his medal at Verdun!*
*He will know what it means and it might frighten him enough to let you go.*
*Paul*

Vacancies were still being advertised at Betteshanger Colliery in Kent, there was obviously something amiss or they would have filled all the places by now, but it was a start. When he told Alice about the development and what he planned to do she insisted on giving him £25 for the fare and to tide him over until he got a job.

When the reply came it wasn't from Thérèse but Maurice, quite long and in French. Alice knew enough French to get most of the message. "It's from her husband and it's very unpleasant" she said, "the parts I don't understand are probably not words they would have taught us. Some child gave your letter for his wife to him and he opened it. It is saying keep away from my wife or you are both going to regret it. She doesn't know about the letter and the person you mentioned is dead and wouldn't have been believed anyway. What's the last part about?" When he had explained about Jean's informant, she said "He sounds dangerous, you are going to have problems with this man, especially now that he knows."

He couldn't see any way out now apart from going to Carvin and taking his chance with Maurice. Sarah was at her mothers again; it was becoming a regular routine for her to stay one or two weeks there, particularly after they had an open disagreement. It wasn't overt running out, some excuse would be made, and he would agree she needed to go, but they both understood. It was a good opportunity to raise what money he could without having to explain. After selling his tools and fishing rods he pawned the only other thing of value he had, his fathers watch. He collected his wages and drew his savings from the Christmas club, it wasn't a lot, but it was all he had and would tide her over until she got a job or went back to her parents. He didn't know what she would do but there wasn't an easy way of doing it.

He decided to stop off to see her at her parents, tell her and go straight from there to France. While packing he came across the accounts book and paperwork from his dealings with Henri Masson. He was about to burn them but thinking about the first book keeping session made him hesitate and then he had an idea and put them in his case instead. He was almost ready to go when a postcard from France arrived and it was in Thérèse's tiny handwriting. Only one line and unsigned it said *'Sylvine is dead'*.

There wasn't going to be time now to see Sarah. He had had five years to tell her and he hadn't done it, he tried to write a letter but couldn't think of anything to say so he just wrote;

*Goodbye Sarah*
*I am sorry we couldn't help each other more.*
*I won't be coming back.*
*Start again if you can.*
*Paul*

He left the cash on the kitchen table with the note and left. Knowing he was going to need language help, he quickly wrote to Jean, telling him that he was coming but was unsure exactly when he would arrive. Hoping it would precede him, he posted it at Victoria station.

Travel in France was now even worse than in the first

days of the war. The armies were still using ferries and railways and there were long diversions around the worst of the devastation. After two days and still nine miles from Arras where Jean now lived, he found it easier to walk rather that wait for another train that was a day late already. To save getting lost in the wilderness of ruined villages, he chose the most direct route which was along the railway line and since no trains passed him it was clear it had been the right choice.

Jean's address was not far from the station and he found it easily. The apartment was one of the few standing buildings among the ruins. On the second floor the door was opened by a young woman who seemed to be expecting him, she introduced herself as Henriette, Jean's wife. He hadn't known about Jean's marriage but he did remember Henriette as the pretty girl Jean had been courting before the war. She spoke enough English to explain that they had received his letter only that morning, that Jean was at work and it would be about five hours before he was due home.
He cleaned himself up in their tiny bathroom, ate some bread and soup, fell asleep, and didn't wake until Jean arrived. Now twenty-two he thought Jean looked much older, but although he limped he seemed to manage well with his artificial foot and didn't use a stick. His hopes for an engineering career were on hold for the moment and he had been glad to get a clerical job in the Mayor's office of the Commune. He didn't want to talk about the war and Paul was glad, he had been safely away from it and felt uncomfortable with its victims.

Jean wanted to know what he intended to do and how they could help. Paul explained "I am going to take her away with me, I haven't decided where we are going yet, could be America or Canada if this idea I've had, works." He got the folder out of his case and handed it to Jean, "This is risky and I don't want you in any trouble, if you could just tell me if it's possible, I will do the rest. There was nearly ten thousand Francs left in the account we had at The Amiens Mutual Bank before the war, I am wondering, if it is still there, could I draw it out now?"

Jean thumbed through the papers before speaking "You would get into trouble if they caught you, but you still have the letter of authority and Masson probably left in too much of a hurry to cancel it. He hasn't got any use for it now and with a bit of luck there won't be any of the original staff at the bank, I bet most of them are dead. Let's give it a try and be ready to run if they are suspicious." Talking of running with an artificial foot seemed to amuse Jean, but Paul insisted "You won't need to run because I will go in, but I might need somewhere to hide if it goes wrong." "OK but let me ask around first about these old accounts, there is no point trying if the Germans got to it first" said Jean.

When they discussed the best way of getting Thérèse away, Jean suggested since Maurice was expecting him it would be better for Henriette to go to the school and get her to leave while he was at work. Paul was unsure about getting her involved but Jean said "If he saw you he might have you locked up on some pretext. The Gendarmes are expecting him to be Mayor soon so they would go along with it and I am not sure how good the Army story will be now with the witness dead."

Next day Jean made general enquiries on behalf of a non-existent relation who had left money in an occupied zone bank. The answer was promising. If the bank concerned had its headquarters outside the zone, the account would be OK and the Amiens Mutual was such. Jean persuaded him not to contact Thérèse until the money issue was sorted out one way or another, after she had left Maurice they would have to leave quickly. He didn't want to involve Jean, but knowing speaking English would draw too much attention to him at the bank, reluctantly he agreed to let Henriette go with him and do the talking.

At the bank, as predicted, there was no one he recognised. She presented the letter of authority to a clerk who took it to the Manager. They were called in to his office and it was explained that for a dormant account he would need authority from his head office. They should return the following day and if they were happy to withdraw part in cash, he suggested Two thousand Francs, they could withdraw the cash then and the balance as a bank draft. However if they wanted it all in cash it would be three days. Henriette agreed to the cash and a draft and without understanding, he nodded in agreement. Outside, Henriette explained it all and was quite excited to be taking part, he just worried what might go wrong. The Bank Manager hadn't seemed suspicious, but not wanting draw further attention to themselves in Lens they caught the next train back to Arras.

Thérèse's classroom was one of a group of temporary buildings, hurriedly erected on the site of the old school. As the children returned noisily from their mid morning break, Henriette followed them in counting on the noise to prevent them hearing what she had to say. Thérèse didn't know her and was just about to ask her her business, when she moved close to her ear and whispered "There is an Englishman outside for you, make some excuse to get away and leave as quickly as you can!" Thérèse looked shocked, but nodded and Henriette left. She walked as calmly as she could to the alleyway opposite the school where he was waiting.

They had waited an hour after the bank opened not wanting to look too eager and although there had been no difficulty, he still expected to be arrested any moment. Henriette said quickly "She will come, I will wait for you at the station." She was about to go when he passed her the envelope with the money and said "No take this and go home, we will follow you, it will be safer." After she had gone he thought about what he had just said, 'we will follow' it seemed hardly possible to be so close now after five years.

It was about fifteen minutes before she came through the school gate but it felt like hours. The headmaster had been unwilling to excuse her until she insinuated that the nature of her illness couldn't be discussed with a man and embarrassed him into agreement. He saw her first, she looked older and had more grey hair, he had been feeling nervous about the reunion but had no doubts now, it was right. When she did see him she walked over to him steadily, fighting the impulse to run. They stood and looked at each other and then shook hands not daring any other display. She spoke first "I knew it was only the Germans keeping you away, let's go!" He immediately thought guiltily about Dorothy but decided it would keep, then he realised that she hadn't even asked where they were going. "Can we go straight to the station or do you want to risk going home for your things?" he asked. "Maurice is at work, how much time have we got before the train?" she asked and when he replied "About an hour now we have missed one" she said "That will be enough." They walked to the house on opposite sides of the road and went in separately.

The house was very different to the one he had remembered, German soldiers had seen to that, but he didn't have much time to reflect on it. She shut the kitchen door behind him and began kissing him, he struggled out "Have we got time?" "Yes this is more important than packing" she said but it was only a moment later when they heard the door and Thérèse facing it saw it open, it was Maurice.

Somebody at the school had sent a child to the Town Hall with a message. She let go and Paul turned round to face him, he saw his eyes switch between them then fix on Thérèse. It was only a moment but it was his chance, Maurice was bigger than him but growing up in pit villages had taught him at least one lesson, get in first. He brought his knee up between Maurice's legs as hard as he possibly could and when his head snapped forward, he butted him in the face. Maurice dropped to the floor and writhing with pain and bleeding from a cut over his eye, began shouting at them. Thérèse shouted back and Paul stood ready should he get up. Suddenly she ran out of the room and came back with a school hand bell. Instead of hitting him with it as he thought she might, she began ringing it. Then there followed more shouting from Thérèse until he went quiet except for groans of pain and she said, "I will pack now, just watch him I won't be long."

Ten minutes later they were walking away from the house and Maurice didn't follow. They had a nervous wait at the station and it wasn't until they got on the train that he discovered what had been said and why she still had the bell. They were the only passengers in the carriage, with no one to overhear she said "He was threatening to put me in a lunatic asylum, I threatened to ring the bell around the town until I had an audience, then tell the world that I had been a virgin until I found a lover after four years married to him." He was still puzzled "Why did that stop him?" "He wants to be Mayor, Frenchmen will forgive almost anything even the little boys, a mistress would have got him even more votes, but there is not a Frenchman alive who would vote for a man who had never done it with his wife!" He was lost in admiration and said "I just hope the bell frightened him enough to let us get away." Then for the first time she said, "Where are we going?"
"America, Canada, or Kent. Take your pick!"

On the way to Arras, they went over the happenings of the last five years. He described the events of his return home in 1914, the intercepted letter and the eventual loss of Dorothy. Her story began with a shock for him; when she told him of the miscarriage she suffered on the flight from the Germans and the surprising if short-lived kindness from Sylvine. The four years as poor relations in Dijon she skipped over and said it could wait for another day. He was deeply shocked that but for the war he may have found himself torn between two pregnant women. With no idea what he would have done, it came as a relief when they arrived in Arras and the problems of the present.

Jean was at work and Henriette was waiting alone for them at the apartment. She was visibly relieved; her excitement had turned worry when they had missed the train. That evening they all celebrated with the best food and drink Henri Masson's money could buy. They spent the night on the sofa and refusing Jean's offer of further shelter, left in the morning for Cherbourg .

# CHAPTER 8

## NEW WORLD

In Cherbourg they joined the masses from every corner of Europe, all using any means legal or not, to arrange documentation and passage to the United States or Canada.

Paul had a passport, Thérèse hadn't and it took more of Henri Masson's money than they would have liked 'greasing palms' to overcome it. Having booked 3rd Class to New York they lived as frugally as possible whilst waiting 3 weeks for the sailing. To avoid problems at immigration, they wanted to arrive in the US with enough to support themselves for a time. It was an uncomfortable journey, made even worse by having to sleep in 'shifts' after foiling an attempt to steal their remaining cash.

They didn't have too much trouble with immigration; healthy and with funds to support themselves they were, compared with many of their fellow passengers, allowed through fairly quickly. Temporary permission to stay had been given conditional on Thérèse sorting out some irregularities with her documents at the French Embassy. As her documents were very irregular, this they ignored and it turned out later to probably have been a wise decision.

They found a shared room in an apartment block and with enough of Masson's money left and casual work most days, he felt it was time to repay Alice. He wrote assuring her they were safe but not settled and expecting more moves. Thérèse wrote to Jean along the same lines, however he quickly replied with rather worrying news.

*Dear Friends.*
*Glad you are safely away but I have some news that you need to be aware of. Last week I had a visit from the Gendarmes wanting to know your whereabouts. It seems Maurice, had gone to them trying to cause trouble for you both and I don't know how but, the visit to the bank and the money had come to his notice. The Gendarmes seemed bored and not very interested in a runaway wife but they were in the money. They came to me because Maurice knew I had worked with you at the mine. They don't seem to know who the woman with you at the bank was. Henriette was staying in the country when they called and was never mentioned by them. I denied any knowledge and I think convinced them I have had no contact with you since the outbreak of war. As they left I overheard Cherbourg mentioned, I assume the draft was cashed there and from that it wouldn't be too difficult to work out where you had gone. I wouldn't think they would search America such a sum but I do think you would both be wise to keep away from authorities for some time.*
*Your friend Jean*

Thérèse's papers wouldn't have stood scrutiny at the Embassy and although unlikely that French police would be looking for them here, it was another good reason to keep away from it. New York was not for them and this decided it, they would go and lose themselves in a big country.

The coal mining districts of Pennsylvania seemed the logical place to look for work and he soon found a job in his own trade at a colliery in Bridgeville. However, in spite of paying well, the working conditions and bullying managers made Nottinghamshire look positively good and gentle. He tolerated it for a few weeks but when a railway company advertised vacancies for engineers at their depot in Pittsburgh, he applied and was accepted. The pay was less but conditions better.

He must have impressed as he was asked, after just a few months to move to their depot in Rochester New York State. He had little option but to agree as it wasn't really a request, but when they arrived there it was to a pleasant surprise. Rochester, bordering Lake Ontario was cleaner, quieter and an altogether nicer place that felt like a good place to settle. The work was interesting, conditions good and if this was to be his lot, he was more than happy. Thérèse was also in a good position to earn; being close to Canada, local companies often dealt with French Canadian customers. This not only provided a steady stream of translation work for her but also students wishing to learn or improve.

Just two years after their flight, life was good but

while rarely spoken of, thoughts of Sarah still troubled them .

## Buffalo, New York State, April 1921

As the train pulled out of Buffalo station, they sat facing each other on the window side of the carriage hoping for a last glimpse of the Niagara Falls from their side. It had been a good day and they both wanted to make the most of it. When the conductor came to check their tickets, Paul showed him the company pass. Every time he did this he was so glad he had found the job with the railway company, with the free travel they often had trips like this.

They had been sitting quietly for some time when Thérèse said "Each time we have a lovely day like this I start thinking about Sarah, she won't run away and live with another man while she is still married to you, will she." He agreed but didn't understand where it was leading and was glad when, without saying any more about it, she changed the subject.

## May 1923

Paul had been working an early shift and got home to their apartment just after midday, Thérèse was in and looking very pleased with herself. "Close your eyes" she ordered, "I have a surprise for you." Thérèse's surprises usually had to be taken in the bedroom, so when instead, she put an envelope in his hand, he actually was surprised. "You are officially dead now" she laughed. The envelope addressed in Jean's hand contained an official looking paper in French. "It's a Death Certificate, when I found out Jean handled death registrations in his office I asked him if he could do it. That was nearly two years ago but it has taken him until now to manage it." He must have looked confused because she said "Its for Sarah!"

Jean had been keen to help, but being found falsifying a Death Certificate would have cost him his job and more. The opportunity presented itself in January 1922; a shaft deliberately destroyed by the Germans at Dourges No 2 mine before their retreat, had collapsed while it was being reconstructed. Along with eight local men a number of foreign workers had also lost their lives. The foreigners were mostly rootless types, unlikely to be missed in their own countries and had included at least two English. Working on a casual basis for a man who had also been killed, their identities were in doubt, and as the bodies had not all been recovered, so was the exact number. When a list made out on the basis of affidavits passed through Jean's office; it had not been difficult to add another name.

Paul was now officially dead. They agreed that Sarah was entitled to know the truth, leaving her to decide whether to use it. Thérèse persuaded him to let her to write to Sarah, offering her the certificate. He wasn't convinced but she said, "If it was me, I would prefer to think badly of another woman, than believe you had run away from me." This was only partly true, she felt guilty about Sarah's situation and secretly hoped she might be forgiven if she was the one who gave Sarah a way out .

# CHAPTER 9

## SARAH

### March 1919

When Sarah had tired of her mother and returned home, Paul had already been gone two weeks. She was worried and angry but not particularly hurt and strangely not very surprised. In spite of the note, she waited a week to see if he would return before she went to see Alice Maynard. He had been close to her and if anybody knew where he was it would be her.

She came away from the Maynards sure that Alice knew more than she had admitted. She had resented their friendship and having made that obvious, they were not close enough now to discuss why he had gone. Alice had evaded the subject and managed instead to talk about the practical implications of what Sarah might do. She suggested that, in the short term, she could explain his absence by saying he had recalled to the unfinished job in France. This had been a major worry to her and she gladly took up the idea, people would soon lose interest and it would give her time to think about what to do next. The immediate future could only be returning to her parents and eventually finding work.

Her return had not been welcome; her mother looked on it as a social disgrace and failure on Sarah's part, what her father thought she didn't know. She also began to see how her upbringing had been responsible for her trouble and bitterly resented her mother's part in it. Finding a job wasn't going to be easy, even with her fathers influence she soon realised she wasn't qualified for anything but service or return to the hosiery factory and she didn't want either.

In spite of her earlier antipathy, she turned to Alice rather than her parents for advice. Discussing what sort of job she might do, Alice, who knew she was no fool, suggested clerical work. It had been the preserve of men before the war but more women were getting it now and although she had left school at fourteen, she could train. She didn't take up Alice's offer of a loan for the Commercial College, she was still able to manipulate her father enough for that, but did borrow her typewriter for practice.

Two years almost to the day after Paul left; she started work at the Mansfield Co-operative Society Head Office accounts department. The Coop didn't employ married women so she became a widow that day.

June 1923

When Sarah came in from work her mother couldn't wait to press the letter in her hand and say, "Who do you know in America?" She couldn't think of anybody, but seeing how curious her mother was, she said, "I can't think just now!" and went to her room to read it.

Since she had been forced to return to her parents, hardly a day had passed when she hadn't regretted the outcome of her marriage. Withholding the contents of her letter was one little way of getting back at her mother for the constant interference. She read and re-read the astonishing letter. It was short and it came as a bombshell. Without a return address, Thérèse had written:

*Sarah*
*Paul is with me and we are very happy.*
*This document might help you have the sort of fresh start I was lucky enough to have.*
*It is an official French Death Certificate, certifying that he died in France last January in a mine accident along with a group of other men. There was doubt about who they were and the bodies were never recovered so I think it would be safe to use.*
*You could be single again if that is what you want.*
*I know it cannot have been be easy for you.*
*Please try to forgive me sometime.*

*Thérèse Delmas*

She had never considered that another woman was involved, but the name Delmas leapt out and then she understood it all. However as Thérèse had predicted, she felt better for knowing. She certainly wanted to use it and she already knew who with.

The only question in her mind about the certificate was 'could she get away with it'. Paul and this woman were not going to expose her, but still she worried about the consequences if found out. She really wanted to talk to somebody and wracked her brains trying to think who she could trust, ruling out friends and family, she decided to talk to Alice.

It had been some time since she had last seen her and it was obvious that the strain of looking after Maynard had taken its toll, but she seemed pleased to see her and took her to the front parlour where she Paul had often talked over whisky.

Sarah decided to be completely honest, without further explanation simply handed her the certificate and Thérèse's letter then said, "Nobody else has seen this. If it were you would you do it?" After the moment it took to read Alice replied "In your position I wouldn't hesitate, nobody who knows is going to talk and without that letter nobody could prove you knew either."

To Sarah's astonishment she then told her what she had told Paul years before, about herself and Maynard. "So for over thirty years I have lived with and had a child by a man I am not married to. You have real chance here, I only wish we could have got away with something like that, but too many people knew." She reached for the whisky and Sarah accepted a small measure. Alice continued, "I don't suppose the man you have in mind; there is one I assume" Sarah nodded "would go along with bigamy or even just 'living in sin'." Sarah said, "I am not certain but no I don't think so, he is going to get on in the world and it wouldn't do." "Well if you can live with keeping this to yourself, you should do it, you deserve some happiness."

Alice hesitated, "Now I have a confession. I helped him go, and know he is in America or he was when he returned money I lent him but I have heard nothing since." She felt she ought to have been angry but having long suspected that Alice knew more than she had admitted, it wasn't much of a surprise. After hearing what she herself had done, it made sense that she would have helped him as she was now willing to help her.

Sarah said "You are right and I am not going to get a chance like this again but my parents, especially my mother could be a problem. They know I pose as a widow for my job but she isn't going see me move on and get married again unless she believes its genuine. It cant just appear out of 'fresh air' . This letter from America is the first letter from abroad that's ever come to our house and she might well connect it ."

Between them they devised a 'cover story' about a French Coal company and postal delays but since her mother would see the post before her most days it needed to appear to have come from France. At this point Alice said "I have an old friend from school who married a Frenchman, if I ask her she will send you French postmarked envelope and wont ask why."

When she left, Sarah felt she had a new friend and after their shared confidences, a friend she could trust.

It was a few weeks before the letter from France arrived and as Alice had promised all it contained was a blank sheet of notepaper. She had decided when she divulged its alleged contents, at least a little display of grief was needed for her husband, even though he had deserted her. After a few quiet days and the occasional tear, she was happy the show she had put on had been enough to convince them their daughter was now genuinely a widow.

George Watson had been interested in her since she first started work in his department. He was the deputy head and had his own office raised above the large open office where she worked with twelve other clerks. Occasionally she would glance up to see him looking in her direction from his window, he could not be looking at anyone else, at thirty three she was about his own age and the only eligible woman there.

Later she had allowed him to escort her to concerts at the Floral Hall and had been his partner at office functions but she had kept him at 'arms length'. She knew she could have had him at the snap of her fingers and there could have been others, but still married, there didn't seem much point. Now that she was free to remarry, he was the only candidate. She actually liked him and he was ambitious enough for both of them.

Since leaving the Army he had been steadily working

his way up in the Co-operative Party and had been a councillor for nearly two years. Sarah was convinced he would go far, he was ambitious but careful not to show it or make enemies of people who could be helpful. He was not experienced with women and she decided he would need careful handling if he were not to be frightened off. There was one problem, the date on Paul's death certificate would expose her subterfuge, and she could confess to that much but no more, she was fairly sure he wouldn't go along with bigamy.

Warming up their friendship gradually, she waited for him to make the moves and did not always accept. However after several months like this she saw that she would have to take the initiative if her target of twelve months to be married was to be met. She accepted all his invitations now and while keeping up a show of modesty, encouraged him as much as she dared. Privacy was the problem and they both found this frustrating, especially George. He lived in rooms that a landlady guarded and her parent's home was out of the question. One evening after the cinema, as they kissed in a doorway she took the plunge "We are behaving like children here, I have been a married woman and I am not used to it!" The word she was hoping he had picked up was 'married', she went on "Can't you arrange something?" It was an invitation she knew that he would accept and do something about.

The following week, with some embarrassment he managed to ask her to go with him to Skegness for the weekend. For a moment she considered demanding separate rooms but decided it would look too coy, putting on a show of surprise, she accepted. Booked in to a hotel under an assumed name, she enjoyed the escapade far more than she had expected. They had walked along the front, paddled in the sea, and had high tea in a seafront tearoom. Later they saw a show and had supper in a café.

It was still quite early for bed when she suggested it, but she was impatient to put the last piece in place, he had to propose and accept her confession first. When at last they went to their room, she undressed out of his sight and waited for him in bed. When he joined her, she tried to behave how she imagined a respectable widow would, warm but without appearing like a tart. Guessing he was inexperienced, she said "If you haven't done much of this before, why don't you let me look after things? I am out of practice, but I think I can remember the general idea."

George, fearing a display of his ignorance was relieved and more than willing to go along with her offer. She had got it just right. He followed her lead and took off his night things and then allowed her to guide him. She carried on gently encouraging him, but had to remind herself she hadn't got him quite yet. It was over quite soon and they lay quietly holding each other while she waited. She knew he was going to feel obliged to propose and didn't have to wait long. George was overwhelmed by it all and was only afraid that she might not want to marry him. "Sarah, you will marry me, won't you!" he said. She was ready; in a worried voice she said "Before I say yes, there is something I have to tell you, in case you want to change your mind." She told him the whole story except that Paul was still very much alive.

Expecting something dreadful, he was so relieved he almost laughed, she had been worrying about a trivial lie to get a job, and he loved her all the more for her honesty. Sunday morning he made the first move and Sarah, since they were engaged now, saw no need to hold herself back. Her new life wasn't going to include bedroom campaigns, she wasn't going to repeat that mistake, and anyway, George wasn't going to need pushing. The thought excited her.

In spite of Alice's advice to destroy Thérèse's letter she hadn't done it and the closer the day of the wedding came the more troubled she felt. Her earlier confidence that she could live with it waned the more she found herself not just liking and admiring George but loving him. She had no fear of being exposed but the prospect of living the rest of her life with this secret was too much for her, even if it cost her her marriage she was going to have to tell him.

Two months before their wedding they were again in Skegness and she decided it couldn't wait any longer. They lay in bed and she said, "There is something you need to know before we can get married." The word 'can' alarmed him as his first thought was that she might be pregnant, before he could respond she reached for her bag and handed him the letter. He read it and was silent for what seemed a very long time, then said "Has anyone else seen this?" and when she said "Only Alice Maynard and I trust her", seemingly satisfied he very carefully tore it up into tiny pieces. She couldn't hold the tears back any longer and he just held her close until they subsided. Then he said "Sarah whatever we have to do we'll do it, now lets forget all about it." They never spoke of it again and eventually she almost began to believe the French accident story herself .

## Coop Café, Mansfield, July 1924

Sarah was tired and glad to see that most of the guests had gone and soon she could get rid of her parents. They were going to Scarborough for a few days honeymoon, but not before he had attended an important meeting on Tuesday.

Glad as she was to be Mrs. Watson, it had been a day she would be happy to forget. When the minister had called ' If anyone here present knows of lawful impediment…' her heart had been in her mouth. She had known she was safe ever since the registrar had accepted the French Death Certificate and issued the certificate allowing the chapel ceremony, but visions of a 'Jane Eyre' denunciation haunted her until it was over.

George was sitting with her parents trying to make conversation with her mother Susannah. She went over to their table and ignoring Susannah's glare said, "George come and say goodbye to Aunt Jane!" When they were out of earshot she hissed "You are wasting your time with her, she won't change now, let's get rid of them and go home."

Sarah and her mother had argued so violently before the wedding it had taken a rare show of force by her father to make her attend. The men-folk were unaware of the reason for the argument; her father Fred would never know but she intended telling George at the first opportunity. At first Susannah had been overjoyed at the news and immediately started to remind her of her views on the management of men in marriage. This time not only had she refused to listen but blamed her advice and the upbringing she had given her daughters, for Paul's desertion. She had, with the greatest difficulty, resisted telling her that her father had found it necessary to have a 'fancy woman' and only then for his benefit. To make quite sure Susannah understood she was doing things differently now, she told her she had been sleeping with George for months.

George, looking out of the bedroom window, without turning round said, "What would you like to do on your first day as Mrs. Watson, Sarah?" "Let's have breakfast in bed and then make our own amusement" she replied. She was surprised hearing herself talk like this and for a moment wondered if Paul's new woman said such things. She didn't have time to ponder any more about them, as he turned round she could see he wouldn't want breakfast yet.

They had a carriage to themselves on the 11:40 from Nottingham to York. They were feeling particularly pleased with themselves and glad they had delayed the journey until after Tuesday's council meeting. Sarah was not only Mrs. George Watson now but also wife of the Council Leader.

The Labour and Co-operative group had been in control for under a year but it had been clear for some time their leader wasn't up to the job and showing signs of cracking under the responsibility. When a small group of councillors asked him privately if he would take on the job in the event of a 'coup' he had been unsure. It wasn't certain they would get enough support, if they failed he would be finished and there was also the problem of timing. They were adamant, they must strike now, and it would interfere with his honeymoon plans. Sarah hadn't hesitated, the honeymoon could wait.

She took the parcel that had arrived just as they had been leaving for the station and tried to guess its contents. Feeling around it she decided that it was a book, but from whom? The handwriting wasn't familiar. She couldn't resist any longer and tore off the wrapping.

The book was; 'Wise Parenthood' by Marie Stopes, there was a note inside.

*Sarah*
*I have only just heard about your marriage and am very pleased for you. I hope you don't mind my choice but you might find this useful if you don't plan to fill your new life with babies.*
*Regards*
*Alice Maynard*

"What have you got there? " he asked. She laughed

and handed it to him "A useful present from Paul's lady friend."

# CHAPTER 10

## THE BEST CHANCE

November 1924

When George got home from work Sarah was bursting to tell him about the letter and had to interrupt his account of the bus breakdown that had delayed him, saying "There is a letter from the Ashfield District Labour Party, perhaps you've got an interview! Open it quick I've been dying to know all day." He ran his eye over it "Yes, Yes, Yes!" he said excitedly "Next Wednesday!"

The Ashfield Labour Party was interviewing prospective candidates to replace the one who had resigned after the previous month's disastrous election result. A market town; the electorate was made up of white-collar workers from Nottingham, agricultural workers and some miners from the Derbyshire pits just over the border. It had never elected a Labour candidate before and had just returned a Liberal with an increased majority.

Sarah had persuaded him to apply, pointing out how his political weaknesses could be turned to advantage.

He didn't have enough influence in the unions to be selected for a safe industrial district, but the prospects didn't look good enough to generate much strong competition. Middle class voters would be less threatened by his white-collar background and with several years to prepare the ground; a swing in the party's fortunes could be enough to put him into Parliament.

He became more and more convinced this was the best chance he was likely to get and it had been Sarah who had spotted it. In spite of having no experience in politics, now she knew the rules of the game, she was a very astute partner.

The interviews were being held in large room above The Marquis of Granby pub and they sat in a corridor with the other candidates awaiting their turn. The interview panel was ostensibly selecting a short listed candidate for the full party meeting to consider, but everyone knew this was where the decision would be made. The meeting next week in front of the gathered local party activists would only be a rubber-stamping exercise for tonight's victor.

They had already decided which of the committee to target. The Chairman, a former NCO in the Sherwood Foresters, had to be won over, the Treasurer, who was an economic conservative and a forceful miners union official named Price, they would probably sway the rest.

George was the last to go in but while they waited, he studied the opposition. He only knew one of the three, a foundry man active in the union. There was young "Toff" who looked hardly old enough to vote and an older man with a look of the fanatic about him. *'Keep your nerve and you're in here'* he told himself. When they finally called him, they both went in. After the last election they needed reassurance and he was going to give it them.

There were six men seated behind a long table strewn with papers and overflowing ashtrays. The Chairman stood up when they walked in. "Harry Richardson!" he said offering a hand. George took it and crushed it for all he was worth while looking Harry straight in the eye. "Thanks for coming George." He said and looking in Sarah's direction he added, "I don't recall asking your wife along though!" George, still fixing his stare said "And I don't recall you telling me not to! If you don't mind I shall explain why Sarah is here later, she won't get in the way." He saw the slightest wink from Harry as he said "OK let me introduce you to the rest of the committee."

He knew he had been tested, if he had backed down he may as well have gone home there and then. Sarah sat at the back of the room. He could see from the position of the chairs the previous candidates must have been sitting well back so he drew his chair up close to the table and sat down. Harry introduced the rest of the committee and then said "Tell us a bit about yourself George before we start." He gave them a deliberately brief picture of himself, he didn't want to have to repeat too much detail later, and he said just enough to draw the questions in the directions he wanted.

The questions were much as he expected, the Treasurer was satisfied with his economic views and a mention of Maynard Keynes, whom George suspected he hadn't read either, shut him up. Arthur Price the miner seemed to have been impressed by the show with Harry and wasn't too difficult. George talked about his own Clerical Workers Union and the problems getting of white collar members and it gave him the opportunity to mention 'Working Class and Workers by Hand or Brain'. When Arthur asked about state control of the mines, he talked enthusiastically about safety and brought Sarah's dead husband into the conversation. He had to establish some class credentials and overcome the 'Grammar school, soft office worker' image. Marrying a miner's widow was as near as he was going to get real 'Working Class' with Arthur but he thought it was enough.

There was only one open pacifist, a teacher named Howard and he gambled that upsetting him would probably endear him to Harry so he went for the jugular. When Howard asked him "Do you think workers killing each other for the capitalist system is ever justified?" He said "Not in theory it isn't, but those Huns on the Hindenburg Line weren't throwing Marxist arguments at us when we swam across the St Quentin Canal. We can think about the rights and wrongs of it when the world is Socialist, but until then we need an Army and be prepared to pay for it. Don't forget its working class lads who do the fighting, you wont find me voting to cut their pay or send them out to fight without the best equipment!" He didn't bother to look how Howard had taken this, instead he looked for approval from Harry, and he had got it.

The last question came from Harry, "Mr. Watson, why should we make you our candidate?" It was the only question that mattered and he had wondered if anybody would forget their personal obsessions long enough to ask it. "Because I can win it, there are people out there who don't like us and they have the vote. They are afraid of Bolshevik revolution, pacifists who would abolish the Army or having their semi-detached house confiscated! This constituency has enough of them to keep us out so we need to reassure them. Leave that to me, with my background I won't frighten the clerks and bookkeepers or insult the men who served in the trenches."

Making a point of looking towards Sarah he said "You asked me why I had brought my wife along if you remember. Before long I think its almost certain that the rest of the women will get the same voting rights as men at twenty one; if it does happen before the next election there will be nearly seven hundred and fifty women here who have never had a vote before. My wife will make it her job to get their votes.

Give it to me and with three or four years hard work and a bit of luck we can win it!" Sarah had to stop herself applauding, they were her words but George had been superb, they would have to give it to him now, she thought.

Now Harry asked "Have you any questions for us

George?" and George said "Only one Mr. Richardson, do you really want to win this seat, because if you don't, give it to somebody else!"

They had to wait outside the room with the other candidates while the committee made up their minds. George wondered if he had appeared arrogant or been too pushy, but it was they who were called back in. Harry said "George I am pleased to be able to tell you that we will be recommending to the constituency party , when they meet next Wednesday, that they adopt you as our Parliamentary Candidate. Congratulations!" George shook his hand followed by the rest of the committee, not all of whom looked very pleased.

Later Harry took him aside and said "You did all right in there George, you didn't make many friends on the committee but if you had come crawling, I would have made bloody sure you didn't get it!" then smiling "But I think you knew that! And one more thing, how did you know how many new women's votes there are?" George said, "I made it up, the Army taught me more than just pack drill, we had people like you training us!"

That night they had talked into the small hours about the future and were too tired to celebrate the way Sarah wanted. When the alarm clock rang in the morning Sarah stopped him as he went to get up and said "Instead of going to work, why don't we celebrate a bit today?" He didn't take too much persuading, as Leader of the Council he was often absent from work, and there wouldn't be any questions asked.

The 'new' Sarah didn't reward her man in bed for achievement, he got that already, but special achievement needed special recognition. She hopped out of bed and left the room for a few moments before returning to open the curtains. "Lets throw some light on the situation shall we?" she said and after slipping out of her nightdress came back to bed. "Stay where you are, after last nights effort, I would like to make my contribution" she said. She climbed on top of him. "No arguments now, you lie there and conserve your strength" she said .

Later they lay in bed and again talked about last night's event. Sarah said "What was all that about swimming across a canal in the war? I thought you had been in the Pay Corps." "I really don't want to talk about it Sarah" he said but seeing a hurt look at being shut out said "OK but not now. I have a better idea, we can talk later if you must!" He took her hand and put it where she could tell he was ready for more celebration.

They had breakfast that was so late it became lunch; he thought she had forgotten about the war but after she had cleared the table, she said "Canal George, no secrets!" She watched him push the scorched newspaper into the fireplace when he finished drawing up the fire, and seeing she was still waiting and determined to know, he sat down and said "I was in the Army for over three years and in all that time I only saw a few weeks real action. When the North Midlands Division broke through the

Hindenburg Line, I just happened to be there. It doesn't make me some sort of hero, the real heroes were shot at and shelled for years in places nobody ever mentions now. I don't want to put myself on a par with them that's why I say I was in the Pay Corps.

I didn't queue up to enlist; I just waited until they sent for me. I failed the medical twice because of my Asthma, but the third time, I was passed A1 would you believe? That was January 1917. We went to France in May, the draft should have gone to Ypres but our Battalion had been so knocked about, it had been withdrawn before we got there. I was lucky more than once, I probably wouldn't be here now if I hadn't had my orders changed so many times."

"What about the canal?" said Sarah wanting to get back to the original question. "Well, for some reason, they transferred a group of us to the 4th Army with the North Staff's . We attacked the Hindenburg Line in September 1918 and they gave us the part of it where we had to get across the St Quentin Canal. They are not like the canals we have here, much wider and where we were it was at the bottom of huge ditch about fifty feet deep.

The Germans were in trenches on both sides of it. After they had been shelled for twenty-four hours, Germans on our side of the canal didn't put up much of a fight, but then we had to get across the water while those on the other side shot at us. It was foggy and there was a lot of smoke from the guns or we would have been slaughtered. The lads who couldn't swim had rafts or lifebelts, but I think those of us who swam for it came off better; we didn't take so long. The other side was full of Germans and we had to fight our way up another fifty-foot bank to get out. Once we got past the canal, most of the Germans we met had had enough and started surrendering."

"The Army reckoned it was a great victory, but I think the Germans knew it was all up . I wouldn't like to have been up against an Army full of some of the men we captured; real hard men but not enough of them left and most of the rest were just kids. That was more or less the end of my war. I caught the flu just after that and ended up in hospital; the war was nearly over when I went back to my unit. We followed them back to Germany through the parts of France that had been occupied all through the war, but I didn't see much of them again. Because I had only done a couple of year's service I was kept in Germany with the occupation forces for another twelve months after the war ended."

His mention of occupied France had set Sarah thinking of earlier times and she said "Did you go anywhere near Carvin?" He looked at her curiously "Yes, but what makes you ask?" She instantly regretted bringing it up but said "Oh its where Paul was working when he was over there before the war " Then, changing the subject "And what you said to Howard, is that what you really think?" He thought for a moment, "I suppose that's more or less what I believe, I do feel a bit guilty about the way I said it, to score a point with Harry. I saw enough to put me off war for good, but it's not as simple as a pacifist like Howard thinks. I felt sorry for the ordinary Germans after the war; you wouldn't believe how bad things were! The French hadn't got much sympathy for them but it's not surprising after the way they had treated the occupied French. I would like to think they have learned a lesson but from what's happening in Germany now I wouldn't count on it!" Then he said, "Lets change the subject shall we, have we finished celebrating now?"

# CHAPTER 11

## THE FLAPPER ELECTION

Even before George had won the nomination, they knew it would to be difficult to pull off a victory without doing something different and the best hope was to attract the new voters. Although he had plucked a figure for the number of new women voters out of the air at the selection meeting, it wasn't that far off and if and when it happened, they were mostly going to be the of votes of working class women.

Sarah, no longer working, set about recruiting other ladies from the party faithful, councillor's wives and students to work on those who might be voting for the first time. Firstly finding out who they were and working in organisations where they were likely to meet, but the best opportunity came in 1926. Throwing themselves into hardship relief for the families of local miners locked out for nearly six months in the aftermath of the General Strike, they met women almost certain to support the party. By the time of the 1929 election they had an up to date canvas list, it was something none of their opponents had bothered to do.

## General Election Night 1929

At the count Sarah sat with Harry; George was standing on the stage with the other candidates and looking nervous. "What do you think Harry?" she whispered. Harry, who had been prowling up and down the rows of vote counters all night said, "It's hard to tell, but it's going to be close!"

The Returning Officer banged a gavel to call order and started his preamble to the result, Sarah wasn't listening. The Town Clerk, who assumed this role was a self important little man who enjoyed hearing himself speak, he only had everybody's attention when he finally said; "The number of votes cast was as follows, Robert Henry Walters 4521." There was uproar, he was the sitting Liberal member and had obviously lost. It was some time before the Returning Officer could make himself heard but it gave him the opportunity to make pompous threats to clear the hall. "Marcus Joseph Harding 5648 votes." This was the Tory and his supporters stopped the proceedings again with cheers and jeering at the other candidates. Sarah looked at Harry for encouragement but he could only shrug, it was still too close to know. "George William Watson 5869 votes and I declare…" but nothing more was heard. Sarah was on her feet now as was Harry and she threw her arms around him and kissed him.

As the three of them walked the short distance from the Town Hall to Harry's house, it was starting to come light. None of them had slept for twenty-four hours and to save them the journey home he had offered them a bed to catch a few hours sleep. Harry made a pot of tea but Sarah was asleep on the settee before he poured it. Leaving her there George and Harry sat at the kitchen table to drink it, "Majority 221, you know where that came from George!" said Harry lighting a Woodbine. "They have been calling it the 'Flapper' election, so I reckon it's the women" he said accepting Harry's offered cigarette. "Yes the secret weapon, Sarah's women's group and if the others had paid them as much attention, it might have been a different story." "Put the radio on Harry, lets see how the rest of the country went before we turn in."

When Sarah woke up it was almost noon, George waited for her to wake properly "We've won 274 seats and still some more to come! The King has sent for McDonald" he said. Sarah smiled "That's good but have you thought how you are going to hang on to this seat next time?"

# CHAPTER 12

## A POOR STORY

### Mansfield Gazette 1948

Malcolm knocked on the Editor's door and walked in without waiting for a reply. "What do you want me for Charlie?" he said . "Don't you ever wait to be asked before barging in to somebody's office?" he grumbled. "I might have been having a private conversation." That was exactly why he didn't wait but he said, "Sorry Charlie, thought I heard you shout me in, it's a bugger to hear anything out there!"

Charlie knew he was lying but decided to let it drop. "I want you to go and cover the opening ceremony of the new science block at the Mining College tomorrow!" "OK boss, no problem" he said and started towards the door. "Malcolm, I want you fucking there this time, not doing your usual copy, after a word with some secretary who actually heard the speeches, do you understand?" He was about to deny the accusation but Charlie didn't give him chance. "It's being opened by Councilor Watson and I have it on good authority, her twat of a husband is shortly to become Minister of Army Supply or some such fucking thing!" Charlie was always bad tempered but never more so, than when he had to accept that the Labour Party was in Government. "We ain't ever had a minister from this constituency before and even if he's a fucking 'commie' we have got to cover anything to do with him or his bloody wife!" Then for the second time he said "Do you fucking understand, go there yourself and write down what lady fuckin bountiful says and take that bloody photographer with you to get a nice picture of her ladyship with the fuckin scissors in her hand!"

Charlie was always like this and nobody took much notice but as he seemed a bit more worked up than usual he decided he had better attend. The accusation that he wrote many of his reports without actually going to the event was perfectly justified. It was a matter of professional pride never to attend a school prize giving, meetings of council committees, and the like. He had been reporting on these events for so long he only needed a word with someone who had attended to verify what he had written .Based on his knowledge of the participants, he had on more than one occasion done without even that and it hadn't been detected. He could have done the same on this occasion. He had studied the careers of prominent locals for so long he knew their life history better than they did themselves.

He had started out with ambitions of getting a proper journalist's job away from his hometown but it had never happened. During the Thirties he had been grateful just to have a job, particularly when his wife began regularly producing extra mouths to feed. After the fifth arrived, he accepted his lot and concentrated instead, on making it as easy as possible. Mentally filing away gossip and facts on anyone who appeared to be rising in the world had served him well.

In spite of his decision to attend the opening ceremony, he began mentally composing his report.

*'After a welcome from the Chairman of Governors, Sir Robert Creep and a half hour treatise on modern mining bollocks from the Principle Dr Neverworked, Councillor Watson would say how interested her husband had always been in mining chemistry but he was so busy solving the worlds problems that she had agreed to do it instead and then have to be helped to cut the ribbon and maybe if she drank, into a car afterwards'.*

He mentally apologised for the last unworthy thought when he recalled the Watsons were Methodist and not known for drinking. The following afternoon he and the photographer Bernard, grabbed seats in the new lecture theatre as close as possible to the side room where the refreshments were laid out.

He had observed the Watsons for more than twenty-five years and suspected quite early on that she had been more than just a 'sleeping partner'. George had gone through the Thirties carefully avoiding the political traps that had ruined many a career, never more so than when he distanced himself from the National Government of Ramsay Macdonald but still managed to hang on to his seat.

Sarah had been more prominent than most political

wives and at a local level was almost better known than her husband. She had been on the local council since before the war and also ran Georges's constituency office. With him away at Westminster much of the time she regularly dealt with constituents concerns herself and word had it, usually did it very well. She may even have gone further in politics but for the war putting elections on hold when she had been a favourite candidate for an adjacent seat.

He thought he had already heard all her stock answers covering any occasion, but while still keeping a sharp eye on the refreshment area he took down enough to convince Charlie he had actually attended. Sounding quite sincere she said "I am so glad to be able to open this laboratory that will be training the mining engineers of tomorrow. This country of ours needs coal more than ever. We all know only too well the price that has been paid in the past by miners and their loved ones to get it. Now that we the people own the mines, we are determined that it is going to be produced safely. That will not be possible without our young men attending colleges like this." The speech then returned to the usual platitudes.

Then followed an over-long and effusive vote of thanks from the College Principle Dr Morgan for both attending and for her part in the councils help financing the project. He wasn't taking notes or much notice until Dr Morgan said "I am sure the loss of your first husband in mining must have convinced you of the importance of safety and can we all thank you again for you contribution."

As he passed Sarah on his way to get to the free beer in the refreshment room, he paused for a moment. It was a poor story but thinking the personal angle might maybe make another couple of lines he said, "Councillor Watson 'Mansfield Gazette', if I could just trouble you for a moment, safety of miners is obviously important to you especially given your own loss, was it at one of the local pits?" He thought he saw just the slightest doubt in Sarah, but almost immediately she said "Oh no, not local, it was in France, a place somewhere near Lens I think." He thought that sounded a bit vague for such an important event but before he could ask more she was whisked away by the College Principal. On his way to the buffet he thought, *'Come to think of it now I remember her being a widow when she married George Watson, what a bit of luck that first husband getting himself killed turned out to be for you, missus'.*

That evening his wife Joan insisted he look at a newspaper their daughter Margaret had sent from America. Margaret, much to his displeasure had married a GI and gone to live there. His son in law had gone back to college on a scheme for veterans and to Malcolm's surprise, was proving to be something of an academic. He had gained mention in the Rochester Chronicle for topping his year and there was a photograph of him accepting a prize. He glanced at the item and was going to mutter something complimentary to please Joan when a name in another column caught his eye. Paul Blackburn Belcher, his mind raced *'Why does that name ring a bell?'* Few local people went through life so anonymously that their name wouldn't have been scribbled in his shorthand book sooner or later. Inquests, Magistrates, or family celebrations, he would have seen it. It came to him *'I think that might have been her 'ladyship's' name from her first marriage.'*

As the office junior he used to report on weddings and funerals if the parties had any sort of public status such as councillors. It was an unusual name; there couldn't be many Paul Blackburn Belchers about, he read the report all the way through now.

**Coroner's Report Blames Faulty Heater for Death of Local Couple**
**At the inquest held on February 12th into the deaths of Paul Blackburn Belcher 60 and Thérèse Delmas 66 of Maplewood Drive Rochester, the coroner ruled that the deaths of Mr. Blackburn Belcher formerly of Nottinghamshire England and Mrs. Delmas formerly of Carvin France was due to Carbon Monoxide poisoning resulting from a faulty gas heater. He went on to recommend ...................................**

He was still thinking about the name similarity when Joan interrupted him. He decided if he remembered tomorrow, to look into it a bit more at the office.

In the morning, with Charlie out of the office, he worked through the back copies and eventually found a cutting reporting their wedding in 1924; he recognised his own work as an 18 year old.

**Councillor Weds**

**Mr. George Watson only son of the late Thomas and Rachel Watson was married on Saturday 5th July to Mrs. Sarah Blackburn Belcher formerly wife of the late Paul Blackburn Belcher, second Daughter of Fredrick, and Susannah Hale. The Groom is Area Accounts Manager of the Mansfield Cooperative Society and a district councillor representing the Cooperative Party in Park Hall Ward. The Bride, whose first husband died in a mining accident, was latterly a clerk in the district accounts department, Mansfield Coop......................**

He looked at the American paper again and thought, " *Unless there were two Paul Blackburn Belchers and that's bloody unlikely, there is a story here and the old lady being French is just too much of a coincidence. If Sarah wasn't a widow, our new lord and master is married to a bigamist, if what I think is right.*"

Still thinking Sarah had been a bit vague about the accident location he looked up Carvin in the office atlas and sure enough it was no more than ten miles at most from Lens.

Working for a Tory paper all his life, his enmity to Labour was equal to Charlie's, but the difference between them was, he also held the other lot in equal contempt. However this might be the chance to bring one of them down to size and if it was timed to coincide with Watson getting promoted who could say how far it would go. This was the biggest story he was ever likely to get his hands on, probably make Fleet Street.

He summarized what he knew, Paul Blackburn Belcher hadn't died in any mine accident, he was alive until three months ago in America. According to that inquest he had been there since 1919 and had been there with a woman from that same French town. It was as clear as day, he had run off with a French woman and Sarah had got married on the strength of the pit accident tale.

Knowing that wasn't proving it and he would be crucified if he got this wrong. From the Superintendent Registrar's office he got a copy of Sarah's second marriage certificate that showed 'Condition' as Widow. The registrar told him that a widow remarrying would have to produce a death certificate for the previous husband to allow a marriage certificate to be issued. When he enquired if a foreign certificate would be accepted the answer had been, yes if there was a translation. While he was there he also got a copy of the birth certificate of a Paul Blackburn Belcher born in 1889, that tied in exactly. He couldn't prove Sarah knew her husband was alive, but there was enough to prove Paul Blackburn Belcher had run away with another woman and that she had, knowingly or not, lived with another man she wasn't legally married to for twenty five years.

He decided to put what he had to Charlie now and find out how much more digging he wanted doing before they ran it. He roughly drafted a story that drew attention to the recent death in America of a local man thought to have died a quarter of a century earlier. If they ran that, plenty of people would make the connection with Sarah Watson and draw their own conclusions. That wouldn't be much of a story for the paper though and someone else would soon splash the full tale. A better idea might be to pay the private investigator they sometimes used, to dig further.

He put the draft with the source cuttings in an envelope and went up to see him. Entering the Editor's Office in his usual way, quick knock, and straight in, he said, "Got a minute Charlie? I have got something you might be interested in." Charlie was about to complain about his entrance but decided he would get it over quicker if he just let him have his say. "Yes but make it quick, I am going out!"

He had no intention of making it quick, just so that Charlie could go to lunch at the Golf club. He decided to play him along a bit. "What do you think about telling our readers that one of the leaders of society here about, is married bigamously and has been for years?" The colour drained from Charlie's face. "How do you know about Harry Wa..?" he stopped himself short. Malcolm did not reply and then Charlie turned on his other voice and vocabulary, the one reserved for his betters. This was one of Charlie's many unendearing features, privately educated and middle class to his boots he liked to play the tough foul mouthed character with his juniors but reverted to type when dealing with anyone he regarded as socially superior or if he felt like patronising somebody.

"Sit down Malcolm, I don't really think it is the type of story a provincial paper like us should be running. We have a role in preserving decency and respect for our leading citizens. It's not for us to provide shop girls with a giggle at the expense of people they should be looking up to. I don't know who told you about Harry Walesly, but I think it's a 'let sleeping dogs lie case' don't you? You must have put a lot of effort into this and I really appreciate it. Tell you what, why don't you let me buy you lunch and perhaps we could get a round of golf in later."

He was stunned; Charlie was panicking because he thought Harry Walesly OBE JP, one of his Rotary Club cronies had been rumbled . Thinking quickly he said "Ok boss, you're probably right but I thought I should tell you in case somebody else got wind of it, let me go get my coat and I'll meet you outside." He wasn't going to refuse lunch and the afternoon off, courtesy of Charlie.

As he went back to his desk he toyed with the idea of telling Charlie who the subject was but then thought, *"Fuck you, you snob. If you can cover up for a bastard like Harry Walesly, why should I give you the chance to bugger her life up"* and as an afterthought, *" but never mind, sooner or later you are going to regret giving me the Walesly story"*

He had to walk through the print room on his way out. As he passed the cast iron stove in the middle of the room; he lifted the lid, dropped in the envelope, and closed it.

# The End

Printed in Great Britain
by Amazon

60202374R00068